"Are You Ready?"

Rosie nodded yes and stared at Mr. McKernan.

Rosie spelled *extraordinary* correctly.

Carlotta spelled *science* correctly.

Rosie spelled *serious* correctly.

Carlotta mispelled *spaghetti* s-p-a-g-e-t-t-i and Mr. McKernan rang the bell.

Rosie knew that now was the time to use her "Winn technique."

She took a deep breath. Then she closed her eyes and tried to picture how the word looked—what letters were in the word *spaghetti*.

Suddenly her stomach rumbled and all she could see was a giant plate of piping hot spaghetti and meatballs. She couldn't see any letters at all!

Books by Robie H. Harris

Rosie's Rock 'n' Roll Riot
Rosie's Secret Spell

Available from MINSTREL Books

ROSIE'S
SECRET SPELL

ROBIE H. HARRIS

A MINSTREL® BOOK

PUBLISHED BY POCKET BOOKS

New York   London   Toronto   Sydney   Tokyo   Singapore

A MINSTREL PAPERBACK *ORIGINAL*

A Minstrel Book published by
POCKET BOOKS, a division of Simon & Schuster
1230 Avenue of the Americas, New York, NY 10020

Copyright © 1991 by Robie H. Harris
Interior illustrations copyright © 1991 Robert Tanenbaum

ISBN: 0-671-67932-5

First Minstrel Books printing May 1991

10 9 8 7 6 5 4 3 2 1

A MINSTREL BOOK and colophon are registered trademarks of Simon & Schuster.

Cover art by Bob Tanenbaum

Printed in the U.S.A.

This book is dedicated to
all the wonderful kids and grown-ups
associated with the Scripps-Howard National
Spelling Bee, including:

- Reta Rose of the Scripps-Howard National Spelling Bee and Carol Matzell of *The Patriot Ledger*, who "got me going" by answering all my phone calls and letters and providing such wonderful material, over a year's time.
- Evelyn Wall, who even took me out to lunch and set me up with the most talented elementary school teachers.
- Becky Bryant, Nancy Roberts, and Robert Griffen, who allowed me to visit their exciting classrooms, and to their awesome students, too.
- Lisa Ishimaru, the lovely and talented student who allowed me to chat with her about soccer, and her friend Molly Evangelisti of *The Sacramento Bee*.
- Mary Curtin Brooks, who greeted me at the Scripps-Howard National Spelling Bee and made me feel so welcome.
- Sondra J. Austin, who provided me with a seat right up front at the Scripps-Howard National Spelling Bee.

And to

- Kathy Clem, for helping me find out about spelling bees, and for all her wisdom about spelling and reading.
- all the extraordinary teachers who have taught my two children, Ben and David, over the years.

v

Dedication

- my wonderful friends, Liz Levy, Robyn Heilbrun, Lilla Waltch, Trudy Goodman, Debbie Chamberlain, and Sukey Rosenbaum for all their help.
- Ellen Pinzur, for her help with all those words, especially *antidisestablishmentarianism* and *vindaloo,* and to Dee Dee Sheedy for helping me put it all together and for sending it OUT!

And to

- my husband Bill, and to our family friend, Ted Mermin, for telling me that I should go to Washington— even though I thought my book was finished (it wasn't)—to see the National Spelling Bee firsthand.

Most of the words and the description of the poster on page 25 were taken from *The Patriot Ledger*'s (Quincy, Massachusetts) poster for classrooms for the 1989 Scripps-Howard Spelling Bee.

Most of the spelling bee words in this book have been taken from the Scripps-Howard National Spelling Bee's 1988 and 1989 *Words of Champions,* as well as from computer printouts from the National Spelling Bee.

Contents

ROSIE'S
SECRET SPELL

Chapter

1

My New Loo-ook

"I wish I were still in bed," muttered George Davidson as he poured himself a glass of orange juice and sat down at the kitchen table.

Mrs. Davidson sipped some coffee and read the newspaper while Mr. Davidson mixed the pancake batter.

"I wish vacation weren't over. It's so-ooo long until summer," moaned George.

"Only two months and tw-wenty, tw-wenty-one days exactly," trilled Rosie as she stood at the kitchen door and twirled around on her toes. "But who's counting?"

Mrs. Davidson looked up from the newspaper and stared at Rosie. Mr. Davidson flipped a pancake and then turned to take a good look at Rosie.

Rosie stopped twirling. "Well, how do I loo-ook?" she asked in a very loud and high voice.

No one answered.

1

"Knock, knock," said Rosie. George groaned.

"Who's there?" answered Mr. Davidson.

"Orange juice," answered Rosie.

"Orange juice who?" asked Mrs. Davidson.

"Orange juice going to talk to me?" squealed Rosie. George covered his ears and groaned again.

"How *do* you like my new loo-ook?" asked Rosie again as she twirled around in another circle.

"My, my," said Mr. Davidson.

"My sister!" moaned George. "How can I go to school with you looking like that! No, no! You can't be my sister, looking like that! What will my gang say?"

"Your gang will love my loo-ook. It's very . . ." Rosie stood still and thought for a minute. She had to be very careful when she talked about George's gang. She never knew when she might need them or they might need her.

"My look is very sophisticated," added Rosie as she sat down at the kitchen table. "That's a word that describes your gang. And me, too, of course."

Rosie Davidson and her older brother, George, lived on Willard Street in Boston. Rosie was "nine and one whole half years old—only one and one half years younger than my brother, George," as she liked to say. George was eleven, "just plain, old, nothing-special eleven," as she also liked to say.

2

Rosie straightened her glasses and glared. "Am I so stunning that you are speechless?" asked Rosie in an even louder voice.

Rosie was wearing a soft pink T-shirt that had a giant hot-pink heart tie-dyed on the front. Rosie's oversize T-shirt was draped over a pair of jet-black-and-hot-pink, candy-striped bicycle shorts. Rosie's bicycle shorts were so long that they covered her knees and hit the top of her soft pink knee socks.

Rosie lifted her foot and dangled it in the air. "Look at my new hightops," she sang. "Loo-ook!" Rosie's hightops were jet-black and, of course, she had laced them with none other than hot-pink laces.

"I can't look," moaned George, covering his eyes.

"Well, I think I look great! In fact, I think you look stupid. Everything you have on is blue, dark blue. Your shirt, your pants, your socks! Blue's stupid! You have no imagination! Blue's so boring! Blue's just blue. You never have any fun!" Rosie couldn't think of one interesting thing to say about blue.

"Vacation was fun, but we have to go back to school this morning," George shouted back at Rosie. "School isn't supposed to be fun!"

"Rosie! George! Enough!" said Mrs. Davidson in a firm voice. "Stop arguing! Rosie, you sit down and eat your breakfast. You look just fine and so does George. You are both free to dress as you please as long as your clothes are neat and clean.''

''Your mother's right,'' said Mr. Davidson as he placed a plate of pancakes in front of Rosie. ''Stop yelling at each other and start eating your pancakes. I made them specially for you guys on your first day back to school after vacation.''

Rosie and George finished their pancakes in silence, grabbed their knapsacks, and kissed their mother and father good-bye.

''Please, no fighting on the way to school!'' warned Mrs. Davidson.

George walked down and Rosie hopped down the front steps, onto Willard Street. They crossed the park, and Rosie skipped by Mrs. Samuels' house.

A narrow, grassy, U-shaped park ran all the way through the middle of Willard Street. Mrs. Samuels, who was seventy-three years old, and her dog Elmer lived across the park from Rosie and George. Even though Rosie had a lot of friends her own age, Mrs. Samuels was one of Rosie's best friends. Mrs. Samuels had named George and his friends the Willard Street Gang because they liked to hang out together in the Willard Street Park—close to the bench Mrs. Samuels sat on every afternoon when the weather was nice.

"Can't you walk regular?" muttered George. "Why are you skipping?"

"What's wrong with my skipping?" asked Rosie.

"What's your hurry?" asked George in a louder voice.

"I want to get to school. I want to see my friends," answered Rosie as she skipped down the sidewalk. Kitty and Linda were Rosie's two best school friends.

"And there's going to be a new girl in our class. I want to see what she looks like," Rosie added.

"I hope she isn't wearing your loo-ook this morning," snapped George.

Rosie could feel the huh-huhs coming on. Rosie always got the huh-huhs when she was mad or nervous. The huh-huhs helped keep her calm, helped keep her from shouting and screaming at George, which she felt like doing a lot of the time. In fact, she felt like shouting at George right now for complaining about her skipping and for insulting her about her outfit.

"Ge-orge, huh-huh!" she said. Rosie tried to sound stern, just like Mrs. Samuels. Mrs. Samuels always took Rosie's side and always scolded George whenever Rosie and George got into an argument. "George, young man, you're annoying me, huh-huh!" stammered Rosie.

"Will you quit those stupid huh-huhs!" shouted

5

George. "They drive me crazy. You drive me crazy! And if we don't get going, we're going to be late to school and it will be your fault and we'll both end up in the principal's office."

"It will be your fault," Rosie shouted back. "That's what I'll tell my teacher and he'll believe me, huh-huh." The huh-huhs were racing all over Rosie's brain. She didn't care if she was late to school. She'd been late to school twice before and nothing bad had happened to her.

Rosie took a deep breath. Then she sighed. She straightened her glasses and put both hands on her hips. "George!" she shouted, and the huh-huh's stopped sliding out of her mouth.

"Yeah?" shouted George. "Yeah?"

"You're a pain in the butt!" shouted Rosie. "You're a royal pain in the butt! You're a stupid pain in the butt!" Rosie felt great. She felt the best she'd felt all morning, except for just before breakfast, when she'd looked at herself in the mirror.

George was speechless. He turned and glared at Rosie. "If you're so smart in the head," he said, "then how come you forgot your knapsack with all your vacation homework? You were so busy thinking about fun, you forgot your work. You'll never grow up. You'll be late, and I'm not waiting for you!"

Rosie stopped skipping. That was the one school

rule she didn't want to break. If you forgot your homework, you had to go to the principal and explain why. Rosie sure didn't want to end up in the new principal's office. She'd heard tales of how scary Ms. Winn was. Ms. Winn didn't look scary to Rosie. But her mom had always told her, you can't tell a book by its cover.

Rosie turned on her heels and ran all the way home. Her purple knapsack was just where she left it—inside the front door. Rosie grabbed her knapsack, ran down the front steps, and almost crashed into Mr. Quirk, the Davidsons' creepy basement tenant, who was just walking to the sidewalk.

"Watch where you run!" he snarled at Rosie as she raced past him.

Rosie ran to school as fast as she could. When she reached school, she noticed that there weren't any kids outside of school. She wondered if she was late. The huh-huhs were returning. She opened the door, slipped in, and ran down the hall. There weren't even any kids in the hall. Rosie knew she was late.

Chapter
2

The Bench

When Rosie reached her classroom, the door was closed. She stared at the door. Mr. McKernan, her teacher, had taped some beautiful photographs of spring flowers—yellow daffodils, red and orange tulips, and white and purple crocuses—on the door. Above the photographs was a note that said "Welcome back to school. Welcome spring!" in bright orange writing.

Rosie really liked Mr. McKernan. He was always so cheery. He was so nice and he had a great sense of humor. Surely he wouldn't send her to the principal's office. She was only a few minutes late. Rosie opened the door. Mr. McKernan turned and smiled at Rosie. The huh-huhs stopped racing around. Rosie knew she wasn't in trouble.

"I'm so sorry you're late, Rosie," said Mr. McKernan.

Rosie smiled back. Now she knew for sure she wasn't in trouble.

"Just before recess I was telling the class that our principal, Ms. Winn, has notified the teachers that too many students have been coming to school late. So, starting this morning, if any student is late three times, that student has to go to the principal and explain why he or she is late. And, Rosie, this is your third late arrival this year."

Rosie wondered if Mr. McKernan was kidding. He did joke around a lot. He made school fun. But right now Mr. McKernan wasn't smiling, and he wasn't joking around.

"Rosie," Mr. McKernan went on, "I'm sorry I have to send you, but that's the rule. Now just skip down to Ms. Winn's and sit down on the bench outside her office and wait for her to talk to you. We'll see you soon."

"But it wasn't my fault, huh-huh," protested Rosie. "You see, Geo . . ."

Rosie could barely skip, let alone walk, down the hall to the bench outside the principal's office. Her knees felt wobbly, and her face felt red-hot. She was terrified. She'd never been inside the principal's office before. She wondered what was going to happen to her. She felt like running down the hall and out the door. Just this morning she had told George that school was fun. Maybe George was right. Today school wasn't fun at all.

Rosie stood and stared at the wooden bench out-side Ms. Winn's office. The bench looked hard and uncomfortable, but Rosie sat down anyway. She felt a little sick to her stomach. What was she doing on this bench? Wasn't this bench for troublemakers?

Rosie looked down at her feet. Her feet didn't even touch the floor. Her legs were swinging back and forth so fast that she shut her eyes and imag-ined that they would swing her right off the bench, out the door, and far, far away from school.

Just then, Lizzie, a member of George's gang, walked by.

"Oh, no," gasped Lizzie when she spotted Rosie. "Ro-sie, what did you do that you have to see Ms. Winn? Poor you . . ." And before Rosie could answer, Lizzie had tiptoed out of sight.

Now Rosie was really scared. Lizzie was the one kid in George's gang who was always nice to Rosie, no matter what. "If Lizzie's afraid for me, going in to see Ms. Winn will be really terrible, huh-huh! Something bad's definitely going to happen to me! Maybe Ms. Winn will make me write 'I'll never be late to school again' in front of the whole school a thousand times until my hand falls off." Rosie shuddered and looked back down at her feet.

Just then George tiptoed by. Rosie could feel her face turn bright red. George was the last person

11

she wanted to see right now. She was really mad
at him, really furious at him. Her legs were swinging even faster, if that was possible. It was George's
fault that she was in this whole big mess anyway.

If George had been nice to her and hadn't teased
her about her loo-ook, she wouldn't have been so
busy getting mad back at him and calling him a
pain in the butt. Then she wouldn't have forgotten
her knapsack and had to race back home and be
late for school for the third time and ended up on
this hard, stupid bench, sitting in front of the
school for all to see. She wondered if she would
be labeled a troublemaker by all the kids now. She
hoped not.

Rosie prayed George would just pass by and not
say one word to her now. She was so mad that she
was afraid if he spoke to her or teased her, she just
might get up and kick him. Besides, she wasn't
even getting a chance to meet the new girl in her
class. Now she'd probably never be friends with
the new girl in her class. Who'd want to be friends
with a troublemaker?

"So school's fun, isn't it, Rosie? Really fun! I
hear Ms. Winn's a real witch. And that she has
witch powers. Norman told me that she even has
a broom—a witch's broom—in her office!" whispered George as he slithered down the hallway.

Rosie knew that witches weren't real. She'd

12

known that since she'd been a little kid. But she still shuddered when George said "witch." She wished Ms. Winn would hurry up. Waiting just made Rosie all the more nervous, and she was plenty nervous enough. Besides, she wanted to get back to the classroom to meet the new kid in her class. She thought it might be exciting to have a new friend.

Rosie looked at her watch. She'd been waiting for five minutes. She felt as if she'd been sitting on the bench for five days.

Rosie looked at her purple knapsack on the bench beside her. The zipper was partly open and she could see her school papers stuffed inside in one big mess. Rosie thought for a minute. She figured that if she could clean out and organize her knapsack and put her papers and books in order, maybe she could take her mind off Ms. Winn and the mess she was in and maybe, just maybe, she could calm down. She knew she had to be calm with Ms. Winn if she was ever going to get herself out of the mess she was in right now.

Rosie unzipped her knapsack and dumped everything out onto the bench. She couldn't believe how many things she had stuffed into her knapsack.

She took out her favorite hairbrush, her foot-long pencil, a bracelet with painted wooden hearts dangling from it, and a bag of chips she had never even opened. Then she took out all her books and notebooks. Then she took out her homework papers. Even though they were crumpled and rumpled, Rosie liked to keep each and every homework paper. She planned to save them forever. Maybe someday, she thought, she'd be very famous and people would want to look at her early schoolwork to figure out if she had always been so brilliant.

Rosie began to smooth out each paper with her hand and slipped each one carefully back into her knapsack. Soon she began to feel calmer, and her legs began to swing more slowly. She didn't feel sick to her stomach anymore.

"Why should I wait any longer for Ms. Winn when I could be in the classroom, meeting the new kid and having fun?" Rosie thought. "If Ms. Winn doesn't have time to see me, then I don't have time to see her. Maybe Ms. Winn forgot." Mrs. Samuels had told Rosie that grown-ups do forget sometimes.

Rosie stood up and slipped the last of her school papers into her knapsack and swung it onto her back.

Just then a figure appeared next to Rosie. Rosie jumped.

"Just where are you going?" asked a tall, blond woman with half-glasses with bright purple frames sitting halfway down her nose. "Are you Rosie?"

"I'm Rosie, huh-huh, and I'm going nowhere, huh-huh," muttered Rosie as she stared up at Ms. Winn. "I'm staying right here."

"Then come into my office so we can talk," said Ms. Winn.

Rosie followed Ms. Winn into her office. Ms. Winn closed the door behind them. Rosie spotted a broom—a long, tall broom with a purple handle in the corner of Ms. Winn's office. George was right. Ms. Winn was a witch! Not a real witch, but a real scary grown-up. Rosie was really scared now.

Chapter

3

An Open Door

Rosie looked around the room. She couldn't believe her eyes. Ms. Winn's desk was a mess. The piles of books and papers on her desk were almost as high as the big, purple glass vase on the corner of the desk. A bunch of beautiful, tall purple flowers were in the vase. Next to the vase were two purple china elephants. Rosie thought the elephants looked a bit weird, but she also thought it was neat that Ms. Winn had so much purple in her room.

"I just love purple too, huh-huh," Rosie blurted before she could stop herself. Rosie hoped Ms. Winn would notice her purple knapsack.

Behind Rosie was a big, soft, lumpy, comfy purple couch, not the sort of furniture you'd expect in a principal's office—not dark, dreary brown or dark, dreary blue like George wore to school this morning.

"Please sit down," said Ms. Winn. Rosie sat down on the couch and Ms. Winn sat down at her desk.

Suddenly Rosie remembered why she was in Ms. Winn's office. She was not in Ms. Winn's office to have fun—to tell Ms. Winn that she loved purple— that purple was her second favorite color after pink. She was in Ms. Winn's office because she was in trouble. Actually, Rosie believed that she was really in Ms. Winn's office because of George.

"I'm in trouble because I had a fight with my older brother," Rosie explained. She wanted to add "and he's a pain in the butt," but she knew better than to say *that* to Ms. Winn.

"And because he was so insulting to me, huh-huh," Rosie went on to explain. "You see, I had to tell him he was rude, and that took a long time, and by the time we got to Mt. Auburn Street I realized that I'd left my knapsack, huh-huh, my purple knapsack, at home with all my books and papers, and so I ran back home to get them, and I was late. That's why I was late to school today!"

Ms. Winn listened to Rosie. As Rosie talked, she could feel the huh-huh's disappearing for the first time since Mr. McKernan had told her she would have to go to the principal's office. "And," Rosie went on, "that's why I was late. Because of George. Whenever anything goes wrong, it's usu-

17

ally George. Older brothers are really a . . ." Rosie stopped herself.

"A pain," said Ms. Winn.

Rosie was shocked. Ms. Winn seemed to understand. And she was even pretty. Just because George had told her Ms. Winn was a witch didn't make it true. George was wrong, dead wrong. Ms. Winn was definitely not a witch . . . well, probably not.

Ms. Winn took off her glasses and looked at Rosie. "Why is this the third time you've been late?" This time Ms. Winn didn't look too nice at all. Maybe George was right about her.

Rosie thought for a minute. Then she stammered, "The other two times were in the winter when there were big snowstorms and our mom and dad told us not to worry about being late. 'Cause some of the people hadn't even shoveled their front walks and it was hard to walk and Mom and Dad told us to take our time and be safe and not be sorry."

"That sounds like good advice to me," answered Ms. Winn. "And I do understand about older kids. I have two older sisters, and even though we are all good friends now, they still treat me like the baby and are always telling me what to do about everything. They still call me Baby Jean, and I hate that!"

18

"Me, too!" said Rosie. "George is always calling me a shrimp, and a twerp, and I hate that!"

"So, I understand what happened to you this morning," said Ms. Winn. "But it's spring now and we shouldn't have any more blizzards, so there's no excuse for you to be late to school. The reason that I don't want you to be late for school is that there are so many fun events happening here this spring. I'm going to announce one of them in the all-school assembly right after recess."

"See," Rosie thought. "George is wrong again. School can be fun. Even Ms. Winn thinks so."

"Now listen carefully. I want to tell you something very important." Ms. Winn put on her purple glasses, leaned forward, and peered at Rosie. Rosie leaned forward, too.

"Rosie, I looked over your school report cards just before you came in. You have lots and lots of S's for satisfactory, only one E for excellent—for math. I want you to keep having fun at school, but it's high time you did some hard work. You can accomplish almost anything you want to—if you set your mind to do so. But it will take work. Do you understand?"

Rosie thought she understood but she wasn't quite sure. She nodded yes anyway.

"And I have a way to help you," said Ms. Winn. "I want you to think of one thing you want to

19

accomplish from now to the end of school in your schoolwork. That's called having a goal. And if you accomplish that goal and work hard at it, I bet you'll get more than one E on your final report card. It might not all be fun, but when you look at all those E's, that will be fun.''

George was right. Maybe school wasn't always fun. Having a goal didn't sound like much fun, either. It sounded awfully serious. The only goal Rosie could think of was to outdo George. And right at the moment she couldn't think of one single way to do that.

''Well, Rosie, I can see you're thinking about having a goal. Now, don't be late again. I don't want to see you in my office for lateness. But remember, my door is always open if you want to come in and talk or need any help with anything. I'll say it again—my door is always open.'' Ms. Winn stood and opened the door.

Rosie grabbed her knapsack. She muttered thanks to Ms. Winn and ran out the door as fast as she could and back to the classroom. Now all Rosie could think about was the new kid in her class. She couldn't wait to see the new kid. But when she got to her classroom, all the kids were gone and only Mr. McKernan was there. Rosie realized it was still recess time and she headed back out the door.

''Wait a minute, Rosie,'' said Mr. McKernan.

"I'd like you to stay in for the rest of recess. There are some math problems on the board—just six long division problems the other kids did while you were visiting Ms. Winn. I'd like you to do them now, and when you're finished, if there's time, you can copy today's bonus spelling words off the blackboard into your spelling workbook."

Rosie walked slowly over to her desk and sat down. She hated missing recess. When she opened her knapsack to find a pencil, she gasped. On top of her school papers were a bunch of papers held together with a big black clip. She pulled out the papers and looked at the top page.

Big, thick letters were written in bright red ink across the top of the first page in someone's very neat printing. The letters spelled TOP SECRET! DO NOT READ! OR ELSE! Below the letters were long lists of words—words that looked to Rosie like they had been printed out on someone's computer.

Rosie began to read through the long list of typed words—words she had never seen before. She wondered whose papers they were. She wondered how the papers had gotten into her knapsack.

She thought for a minute. Maybe Mr. Quirk, their creepy downstairs neighbor, had stuffed them into her knapsack when she left it inside the front door. But no, it couldn't be him. He didn't have a key to their house anyway and he mostly liked to stay away from George and her.

Then she realized that someone must have left the list on the bench outside Ms. Winn's office. Rosie figured that when she stuffed all her papers back into her knapsack, she must have picked up the Top Secret papers by mistake and stuffed them in her knapsack, too. She wondered why anyone in her school would have a Top Secret list. Rosie was scared. She hoped the list didn't have anything to do with the new kid. Maybe it was just some big kid's prank.

George was right. School wasn't fun anymore.

Chapter

4

Something Secret

Rosie did the four math problems—3 into 41, 6 into 97, 8 into 143, 5 into 926, 3 into 7803 and 4 into 9732—very quickly and checked them. They all checked. She was glad she was so good at math. She'd always been good at numbers. She remembered that even when she was little and her mother would give Rosie and George an adding problem, Rosie always got the answer faster than George.

Rosie looked up at the board. There were four bonus spelling words written on the board—*Massachusetts, harmonica, zigzag, treasure*. Even though Rosie could do math problems like a whiz, she had never cared a fig about spelling. In fact, she had no idea why spelling was important.

Whenever Rosie needed to spell a word and didn't know how to spell it, all she did was ask someone else, like her mother or father or even George. George was a great speller. He could spell almost anything. "But who cares about spelling anyway," muttered Rosie as she copied the words as fast as she could into her spelling book.

Rosie looked up and noticed that Mr. McKernan had taped a big red-and-blue poster, with a big red apple drawn on it, to the board. Rosie got up from her chair, straightened her glasses, and walked over to see the poster close up.

Rosie read the poster out loud. "Can you spell *tatterdemalion?* If so, you deserve the apple and you could win a trip to Washington, D.C. Spell *septuagenarian, cupressineous,* and *misericordia* and you may just have what it takes to outspell other kids from your school and other schools around Boston. You can enter your grade spelling bee. Each grade winner will go on to compete in the *Boston Chronicle* Newspaper Spelling Bee, which will be at City Hall Plaza, and the stakes are high.

"First Prize: All-expenses-paid trip to compete in the All-American Spelling Bee in Washington, D.C. for the winner and the winner's family and friends—up to ten people, plus one official person from your school, of course."

Rosie didn't even bother to look at the prizes.

"Wow!" she exclaimed out loud. She sure would

25

like to go to Washington, D.C. If she went, maybe she'd even get to see the president! Rosie remembered seeing a spelling bee winner on TV shake the hand of the president—the president of the United States!

Rosie walked over to the window and looked out at the playground. She looked for the new kid, but she couldn't spot her. All the kids looked like they were having so much fun. She sure wasn't having any fun. And she could never win a spelling bee. George probably could. Why didn't her school have math bees? She'd win one of those easily. And beat George, too.

Rosie wished recess were over. She was really bored. She hadn't even met the new kid yet. She hadn't done one fun thing in school today. The only fun thing she could think of doing right now was to sneak a look at the Top Secret list. But she was sort of scared to look at it. She was glad Mr. McKernan had left the room. Even Mr. McKernan wasn't fun today.

Rosie sat back down and began to read the words on the list.

"Pro-fit-e-role, scram-a-sax, wed-del-lite," Rosie had no idea in the world what these words meant, but she loved the way they sounded. She figured some older kid must have printed them on a computer. But why? Soon she began to read the words

26

very quickly and soon she began to say them out loud.

"Ai-ki-do, bo-cac-cio, can-nel-lon-i, kook-a-bur-ra, scribb-la-tive, yaw-me-ter . . ."

"This is the first fun thing I've done all day," thought Rosie. "This list isn't scary at all."

Just then the end-of-recess bell rang. Rosie quickly stuffed the Top Secret list into her knapsack. Soon all her classmates started streaming in the door and over to her desk.

"You survived the witch!" exclaimed Kitty.

"It wasn't too bad, but it sure wasn't fun!" admitted Rosie.

"We're so glad you're back," said Linda, "and this is the new kid in our class—Carlotta. Carlotta, this is Rosie."

Rosie nodded hi.

"Carlotta's just moved here all the way from New Mexico, from Al-bu-quer-que, however you say it," piped Louie.

"I can spell Albuquerque," boasted Nick.

"I can't even say the word let alone spell it. But I like the way it sounds," said Rosie. "And I can spell Boston!"

"A-l-b-u-r-k-e-r-k-e-e-e!" said Louie.

"Wrong!" said Carlotta. "A-l-b-u-q-u-e-r-q-u-e."

Mr. McKernan rang the bell and all the kids took their seats and soon quieted down.

Rosie looked over at Carlotta. She looked pretty OK. Carlotta had beautiful, long black hair. Rosie thought she looked like she came from out West. She was wearing blue jeans and a pink cowboy shirt. Rosie wondered if Carlotta would be her new friend. It made sense. It was clear that they both liked pink!

Rosie and Kitty and Linda had been friends ever since the first week of kindergarten and they had fun with each other most of the time. But Rosie thought that sometimes having the same old friends could be kind of boring, and having a new friend might be fun, not just for her, but for all three of them.

Mr. McKernan asked everyone to line up for an all-school assembly. Suddenly Rosie spotted Carlotta's shoes—the exact same black hightops as Rosie was wearing with the very same hot-pink laces! Now Rosie was sure that she and Carlotta would be friends. She hoped so.

Chapter
5

Practice, Practice, Practice

Walking down the aisle of the assembly hall, Rosie passed George and his gang.

"You survived," said Lizzie with a smile.

"Barely," Rosie whispered back. Maybe she wouldn't tell George or his gang, even Lizzie, that Ms. Winn wasn't a witch, and that she was really nice. "If George ever gets sent to Ms. Winn, and he could," thought Rosie, "I'll tell him all sorts of wicked tall witch tales about Ms. Winn . . . that she's really mean . . . really nasty . . . I'll scare him to death!"

"Rosie returns from the Wicked Witch of the West," hissed George. Bill and Peter both laughed.

Rosie gave them her biggest, widest smile, and then she trilled, "Hi ya, guys. Having fun today? I sure am!" Then she waved at George and his gang and followed Carlotta, Kitty, Linda, and the rest of her class down the aisle and into the very front row of seats.

Rosie plunked down in her seat and looked up at the stage.

Ms. Winn walked up to the microphone and adjusted her glasses. Rosie adjusted her glasses, too.

"Good morning, children. Quiet down, please," said Ms. Winn to the assembly, and everyone quieted down. Rosie heard Linda whisper to Carlotta, "That's the witch. Rosie just came out of her dungeon and survived. Rosie's one of the lucky ones."

"But I may be under the witch's secret spell. You never know," whispered Rosie with a giggle. Carlotta, Kitty, and Linda giggled, too.

"Girls and boys," Ms. Winn went on to say, "I have a very exciting announcement to make. But first, how many of you have seen the sign, a sign that has a big red apple painted on it? I put one up in each of your classrooms. The sign says, 'Can you spell . . .' "

"Tatterdemalion!" blurted out Rosie before she could stop herself. Rosie slapped her hand over her mouth.

"Good for you, Rosie," said Ms. Winn. "I see you are paying attention. The sign with the apple and the word *tatterdemalion* is the announcement for the All-American Spelling Bee."

A bunch of kids in George's class whistled and clapped.

"Let me explain how the All-American Spelling Bee works," Ms. Winn continued, "because this is the first time our school will participate in it."

Rosie slumped down in her chair. She couldn't believe that a spelling bee had turned out to be the fun event Ms. Winn had told her she was going to announce. Rosie thought that Ms. Winn was going to announce something like canceling classes for an all-school party or an all-sports day.

"This is the way the bee works. Today, in each of your classrooms, your teacher will give you a practice spelling bee, only so you'll know how a bee works. Today's bee is just for practice and really won't count for anything. After the practice spelling bee, your teacher will give each of you a booklet of practice words from the All-American Spelling Bee."

Ms. Winn held up a booklet with a bright red apple drawn on the cover—just like the poster. "This is a booklet of practice words," she explained. "Each one of you should take the booklet home and study it. Next Monday you will have your classroom spelling bee, and the words will come from the practice book, so, the more you study this book, the better you will do. There are some great words in it like . . . let's see . . ." Ms.

Winn straightened her glasses again. *"Bialys . . . flamingo . . . mealymouthed . . . millionaire . . . rhombus . . . scrumptious . . . xylophonist . . ."*

"Wow!" said Kitty. "This sounds like fun."

Rosie winced. Kitty always got 100 percent on her spelling tests and she hardly even studied. She was just a good speller.

"The winners of your class bees will go on to compete against all the kids in our city, and the winner of that bee will go on to Washington to compete against kids from every state in the nation." Ms. Winn was talking very fast now. "And that winner will go to the White House to meet the president! Wouldn't that be exciting?" shouted Ms. Winn as she tossed her head back in the air. With that, her glasses went flying off her nose and onto the floor. Rosie could hear George and his gang laugh.

"Now, quiet down, back there," warned Ms. Winn as she picked up her glasses. "I wouldn't want to ask anyone to leave, would I? Or have to ask anyone to come to my office for a little talk about assembly behavior?" There was silence. "Now, are there any questions?"

Rosie thought for a minute. She wondered how to study for a spelling bee. She'd hardly ever studied for spelling tests because she thought they were really boring. The highest mark she had received on a spelling test this year was 74 percent. George always got 100 percent on spelling tests and even got all the bonus words right. "Who cares that George is such a good speller?" thought Rosie. Rosie knew the answer. She cared.

"There are many, many ways to prepare for a spelling bee," Ms. Winn went on to explain. "Some kids study alone. Others like to find a friend or a bunch of friends to quiz each other. Or, an adult friend is always okay. And my door's always open for help. Don't be afraid to stop in."

"Sure, just stop in and chat with the witch. No way!" whispered Kitty. "Who cares about spelling anyway?"

"No way you need help, either," thought Rosie to herself. "Kitty may not need help, but I'll need all the help I can get. But who will help me? Kitty couldn't care less. Linda's a pretty good speller, too. What about Carlotta? No, I hardly even know her. . . . It's no use. I can never win." Rosie slumped down in her seat even further.

"Whatever you do," Ms. Winn explained, "practice, practice, practice, and you'll be a winner! Good luck to all of you."

Rosie stood up with her class, and they filed out of the assembly. As Rosie passed George, he said to her in a low voice, "So that's what the apple's for, for Rosie the apple-polisher, trying to polish up the new principal, be the principal's pet, answer all the right questions . . ."

Rosie glared at George this time. She'd show him. She'd win her class bee, and then wouldn't George be jealous of her! She'd show him. But how?

Chapter
6

The Loser

Rosie sat down at her desk. She hoped the practice bee would be over soon. She knew she couldn't win, because she'd never spent any time on spelling before.

Rosie looked over at Carlotta and remembered what Mr. McKernan had said on the day before vacation: "Everyone be nice and friendly to Carlotta when she comes from Albuquerque. She doesn't know a soul here." Rosie decided she would invite Carlotta over to her house some day soon.

Mr. McKernan told everyone to quiet down. "I think we'll have our practice bee right now so you can all see how it works. Today, for our practice bee, and later for our classroom bee, you can write down the word on the chalkboard before you spell it, if you want to. Some people think that writing

down the word helps. Some don't. It's up to you."
Rosie wondered which would be better.

"Breaking up big words like *enjoyable* into sylla-
bles, into smaller words like *en, joy,* and *able,*"
added Mr. McKernan, "helps, too."

"First, I'll say the word out loud," Mr. McKernan went on to explain. "And you can ask me to
pronounce the word again, or use it in a sentence,
or read you the meaning of the word." Rosie was
listening hard. She knew she had to pay attention,
even though this spelling bee business was beginning to bore her and the first bee hadn't even
started yet.

Rosie began to chew on her pencil, but she
stopped when she spotted Carlotta looking at her.
She didn't want Carlotta to think she was a creep.
At least Rosie wasn't chewing her fingernails. Carlotta would probably think that was really gross.

"Now," said Mr. McKernan. Rosie sat up and
stared at him. That was the only way she could
pay attention and keep her mind from wandering.

"I want you to say the word out loud first," Mr.
McKernan went on. "Then, if you want to, write
it on the board. Then spell the word, and then say
it again. Do all of you understand how this works?"

Rosie wasn't sure she understood. She was glad
when Mr. McKernan said, "Carlotta, come on up
here and we'll do a practice one with you."

"Okay," said Carlotta in a quiet voice.

"You'll do fine," said Rosie as Carlotta walked by Rosie's desk and up to the front of the room.

"Okay," said Mr. McKernan. "Your word is— now don't worry if you get it wrong, this doesn't count for anything, this is just practice—your word is . . . *Massachusetts.*"

"Oh no," moaned Carlotta.

"It's just practice, Carlotta," said Kitty. Rosie wished she had said that to Carlotta.

Carlotta said, *"Massachusetts."*

"Oh, I forgot to tell you," added Mr. McKernan. "You can start to spell the word over as many times as you want, but the minute you make a mistake, you're out."

"I don't get it," said Linda.

"You can say 'M-a,' " said Mr. McKernan, "then say 'M-a' again. You can start over again and again, but the second you put in a wrong letter, you're out! Like striking out when you're at bat in baseball. You have to sit down and that's it. You'll know that you're out if I ring this bell."

Mr. McKernan picked up the silver bell he always rang when he wanted the class to stop talking. "Are you ready, Carlotta?" he asked.

First Carlotta said, *"Massachusetts."* Then she picked up a piece of chalk and wrote on the chalkboard, *M-a-s-a*. She erased *M-a-s-a* with her sleeve and thought for a minute. Then she wrote *M-a-s-s-a*. Then she stood back and looked at what she had written. Then she added *c-h-u* and then she added *s-e-t* and stood back and looked at all the letters she had written. No one uttered a word.

Rosie wanted to run up to the board and finish the word for Carlotta. Carlotta was taking so long, and it was so hard to wait. How could Carlotta know how to spell *Massachusetts* when she had just moved from New Mexico?

Carlotta didn't finish writing the word on the board. She turned to the class, stood up straight, and spoke in a soft voice.

"M-a-s-s-a-c-h-u-s-e-t," she said. Then she paused and it sounded as if the whole class had gasped. Carlotta started spelling again.

"I can't stand this!" whispered Rosie as she twisted some strands of her hair around and around into a big knot.

"Me neither," Kitty whispered back to Rosie.

"M-a-s-s-a-c-h-u-s-e-t-t-s!" Carlotta blurted out the letters so fast that this time even Mr. McKernan gasped.

"That's correct!" said Mr. McKernan. "I can see this spelling bee business is going to be a load of fun."

"Finally," thought Rosie, "finally we're going to have some fun in school today."

"Okay," said Mr. McKernan. "Now that we all know what we're doing, let the practice bee begin. There are twenty-nine kids in our class. I have numbers from one to twenty-nine in this hat. Everyone come on up here and line up and pick a number from the hat. Then line up according to your number and number one will go first."

When it came Rosie's turn to pick, she couldn't believe her bad luck. She picked twenty-nine. She would go last—last in the class.

"Now," warned Mr. McKernan, "no coaching from the sidelines! Your word is your word and nobody else's. Are you ready?"

Rosie couldn't believe how nervous she was. She couldn't believe how much she really wanted to win! She could feel the huh-huhs returning.

Rosie and the rest of the class stood along the side of the room as each kid walked up to the blackboard and was given a word by Mr. McKernan.

Louie spelled *cafeteria* correctly. Nick spelled *dinosaur* with an *a* where the *o* was supposed to be and sat down.

Mr. McKernan said, "Good try, Nick," but Nick knew it wasn't good enough and so did Rosie.

Linda struck out on *happiness* and looked very unhappy when she had to sit down.

"Remember, this is just a practice," said Mr. McKernan in his most reassuring voice. But all

Rosie could think of when Mr. McKernan said the word *practice* was "practice makes perfect."

Kitty stayed in with *dictionary*. Carlotta spelled *interesting* correctly.

Then it was Rosie's turn. Rosie walked up to the front of the room as fast as she could. She straightened her glasses and picked up the piece of chalk.

"Ready?" asked Mr. McKernan.

"Ready," said Rosie. "R-e-a-"

"No, Rosie," said Mr. McKernan.

"Was that wrong?" exclaimed Rosie. "I'm sure that wasn't wrong, huh-huh, I'm sure."

"No, Rosie, that wasn't wrong," explained Mr. McKernan, "but when I said the word *ready,* that wasn't your word. I was just asking if you were ready for your word, that's all."

Rosie could feel her face flush and turn bright red. The whole class, even Carlotta, burst out laughing.

"That was my fault, Rosie. And it could have happened to any one of you," said Mr. McKernan to the class. "It shows that Rosie was ready to go and couldn't wait. Now everyone quiet down and be fair to Rosie. Are you ready now, Rosie?" asked Mr. McKernan again.

"Yes, huh-huh, yes," stammered Rosie. She hated it that everyone had laughed. She'd show them. She'd show them that she could be a winner.

"Cooperate," said Mr. McKernan.

"Cooperate," said Rosie slowly. Rosie could still hear some kids laughing. "Could you please use *cooperate* in a sentence?" she asked.

"Will the class please *cooperate* and quiet down—so we give Rosie a fair chance?" said Mr. McKernan.

Rosie felt herself blush again as she picked up the piece of chalk again. *C-o-o-p,* she wrote on the blackboard. Then she stood back and looked at what she wrote and quickly erased it with her sleeve.

Then she started again. *C-o-o-p.* Then she stood back and looked at what she wrote again. She was sure she was right, not quite sure, but almost sure—99 percent sure.

Quickly she added *a-r-a-t-e* to the letters she had already written. Then she said out loud, *"Cooparate, c-o-o-p-a-r-a-t-e . . ."* and peered at Mr. McKernan.

Mr. McKernan rang the bell. "Sorry, Rosie. Good try." As Rosie slipped into her seat, Linda leaned over and said, "Oh well, join the losers. You're in good company."

Rosie knew that Linda was being nice, trying to make her feel better, but losing didn't feel nice at all, and Rosie wondered how she could ever win. Rosie hardly heard the rest of the bee, even when

happ

Massachu

cooparate

dict

dinasaur

feteria

Carlotta spelled *flabbergasted* correctly and beat out Kitty, who misspelled the word *elephant* as *elephent*.

Rosie congratulated Carlotta when she came back to her desk. When Mr. McKernan was passing out the spelling bee practice books, Rosie was wondering if Carlotta would ever be her friend, be the friend of a loser. Rosie had to find a way to be a winner! But how? She doubted that spelling was the way.

Chapter
7

A Waste of Time

At lunch Mr. McKernan asked the class to keep the noise down a bit. "And, yes," he added, "please, while we are eating, do not talk with a mouthful of groceries. That will help reduce the noise level in here." Rosie giggled out loud. She loved Mr. McKernan's silly jokes.

Linda invited Kitty and Rosie and Carlotta to eat at her desk. "We can all pull our chairs around my desk and toast Carlotta, the winner. There's just room enough for three losers and a winner."

Rosie wished Linda would stop talking about losing. "I think the bee's stupid. I'm not going to study for it," declared Linda.

"Me neither," said Kitty. "I don't want to get up there and make a fool of myself and feel like a dip."

It was bad enough to lose at the time, but Rosie

wished she could gag Kitty and Linda or at least make them talk about something other than losing. Rosie wanted to change the subject.

"Wait until you meet the music teacher. Her name's Ms. Mermin," said Rosie with a giggle.

"She's no mermaid," added Nick with a laugh, as he leaned over from his desk.

"She's really mean. And so boring and strict. We sing the most juvenile songs, like 'B-I-N-G-O.' I mean we're not in kindergarten," added Louie.

Carlotta listened eagerly.

"She says you learn about the language of music by singing simple songs," said Kitty. "You really have to behave in her class. But her class is no fun without a little bit of mischief," Kitty laughed.

"And she's so vain, I mean, she's always fussing with her hair so it's just right, every piece in place," explained Linda to Carlotta. "She's not that old, but she wears her hair in this tight bun perched on top of her head, and there's never ever a single strand out of place. It looks like a bird's nest." Carlotta burst out laughing. So did everyone else but Rosie.

"And," added Kitty, "she's so vain she never bothers to wear her glasses except when she absolutely has to. She can't see distances—anything, anyone far away from her. So she's always getting everyone all mixed up who sits in the back row and she never knows who is who. It's a riot."

46

Rosie just sat and listened.

"Hey, Rosie," said Linda. "You sure aren't your usual fun old self today. I really mean it. Was the witch so awful?"

"No," she answered with a sigh. "It's George again. He made me late for school. He's the cause of all my troubles today."

Linda turned to Carlotta and explained, "George is Rosie's older brother. Rosie's the only one of the three of us who has an older brother, and sometimes he's not too nice to Rosie. It's really annoying."

"I've got an older brother," said Carlotta, "but now that he's in college, he's finally nice to me." Carlotta leaned over and whispered, "I even think he misses me when he's away at school."

"I can't imagine George ever missing me," said Rosie with another sigh. "In fact, right now I don't miss him at all, 'cause I'm so-ooo mad at him!"

Rosie was glad when Mr. McKernan rang the bell and announced in a booming voice, "Lunch is over. Time to clean up and then line up for music. And don't give Ms. Mermin a hard time like you did in our last music class."

Rosie threw the last of her lunch in the wastebasket and lined up with Kitty, Linda, and Carlotta. "Maybe Carlotta and I could be friends," Rosie thought. "After all, we both have older brothers and are the only two who do."

Carlotta sat on one side of Rosie in music class. Kitty and Linda sat on the other side of Rosie. They all sat in the back row.

"Good afternoon, girls and boys," sang Ms. Mermin as she went over to the window to pull down the shade.

Linda put her two index fingers inside her mouth and pulled her mouth as wide as she could. Then she stuck out her tongue. Kitty pointed to Ms. Mermin. Carlotta started to giggle.

Ms. Mermin spun around as fast as she could.

"Who is giggling?" she asked in an accusing voice.

Carlotta looked terrified.

"Don't worry," whispered Rosie to Carlotta. "She doesn't have her glasses on. So she has no idea who's who. She's blind as a bat without them."

Ms. Mermin took her glasses out of her skirt pocket, cleaned them with a tissue, put them on and peered through them. Then she shouted, "Now, who was giggling?"

Rosie thought a minute. Then she shouted, "It was me!"

"Rosie," warned Ms. Mermin, "one more rudeness like that and you're off to the principal's office."

"I'm sorry," said Rosie as nicely as she could.

48

She sure didn't want to end up in Ms. Winn's office again.

"Why'd you do that?" whispered Kitty.

" 'Cause I didn't want Carlotta to get in trouble on her first day of school," whispered Rosie. But Rosie knew that wasn't quite the truth. The truth was that Rosie had a scheme that was beginning to form in her mind—a scheme she didn't feel quite right about.

The scheme was this: Rosie knew that she had to win her class bee by herself—and she knew that if she studied hard, she could probably do it. But having a good coach was the only way Rosie figured she would have any chance of winning the citywide spelling bee. And she had to win that if she was ever going to get to Washington! She certainly couldn't do it all by herself! Neither Kitty nor Linda were serious enough about spelling to be coaches. And, besides, George had his whole gang to help him out.

Carlotta was Rosie's only chance to win the citywide bee. Since she had just helped out Carlotta, maybe, just maybe, Carlotta might help *her* out. Carlotta was a good speller. Rosie bet she'd be a great spelling coach.

But Rosie knew there was one bad thing about her scheme. First, she'd have to beat Carlotta in the class bee, and that wasn't being nice to the new kid at all. And would Carlotta want to be her coach if Rosie beat her out? Rosie wasn't sure.

When Ms. Mermin sat down at the piano, Rosie sneaked a pencil and a piece of paper out of her knapsack and scribbled a note to Carlotta. "Kitty and Linda and I think Ms. Mermin should win a trophy for having the biggest behind of all the music teachers in the whole, wide world!"

Just as Rosie was about to pass the note, Ms. Mermin struck a loud chord on the piano, stood up, walked over to Rosie, and stared at her.

"Now, Rosie, you've never been in trouble in my class before, so I won't send you packing to Ms. Winn. But today you've kept us from our beautiful singing two times. Really, you are wasting our time—and yours, too, may I add. Why don't you share this note with the rest of the class?"

Rosie slid down in her chair. "Oh, no," she muttered to Ms. Mermin. "I don't think you'd like it if I read it to the class."

"Well, then, Rosie, why don't you stand up and *sing* your note to the class," ordered Ms. Mermin.

"School definitely is not fun anymore, definitely not fun at all," muttered Rosie to herself. She could feel the huh-huh's coming on!

"Either sing it or off to Ms. Winn's office!" said Ms. Mermin.

Rosie took a deep breath and stood up. Then

she sang, "Ms. Mermin has the biggest . . . huh-huh . . ."

"That's enough, Rosie," shouted Ms. Mermin. Her face had turned beet-red.

Rosie scrunched the note up in her hand.

"Now, Rosie," said Ms. Mermin in a quieter voice, "if you can behave yourself for the rest of the class, you can remain. But one more foolish peep out of you and you're off to the principal's office. You've wasted enough of our time! Today, Rosie, you are a total waste!"

All the kids had their hands cupped over their mouths to keep from laughing out loud. Rosie hadn't meant to waste everyone's time. She really felt embarrassed.

Before she sat down, Rosie tossed the note into the wastebasket. She felt like tossing herself in instead. And then maybe someone would come and empty the wastebasket—right now—with her in it.

Since losing the bee, Rosie had felt like a loser. But no one had ever said she was a waste. Wait until George heard about this! She'd never hear the end of it from him—ever. She was glad music class was over.

Chapter
8

O-U-T

After class Carlotta raced up to Rosie.

"Thanks for taking the blame," she said. "You hardly even know me."

"That's okay," answered Rosie. "Why should a new kid have to take the heat on the first day?"

"Oh, thanks again," said Carlotta with a sigh.

"Want to come back to my house after school and play?" asked Rosie.

"I'd love to!" exclaimed Carlotta. "I can call my mom right after school!"

At three o'clock, when Mr. McKernan rang the dismissal bell, Rosie and Carlotta ran out of the classroom, out the front door, and all the way back to Willard Street. On the way home Rosie told Carlotta about the Top Secret list.

As soon as Rosie reached Willard Street, she pointed out Mrs. Samuels' house and told Carlotta all about Mrs. Samuels. Then she charged up Mrs.

Samuels' front steps and sat down on the rocking chair on the porch. Carlotta followed her and didn't say a word.

Rosie wished Mrs. Samuels were home. This was definitely the wrong time for Mrs. Samuels to be out of town visiting her nephews—just when Rosie needed her to help her think straight.

Rosie peered through her glasses and looked over at the park. George and his gang were sitting on the grass. She knew she couldn't cross the park to get to her house just now. She couldn't face George. Not in front of Carlotta. Not yet.

Suddenly Rosie had an idea. Before she could stop herself, she motioned to Carlotta to follow her and she marched down the front steps, into the park, and over to George and the gang. They were sitting in a circle, studying their spelling bee practice books.

"Oh, I see you are all studying for the spelling bee," said Rosie as she slid her glasses halfway down her nose. "How can I help you out?" She wondered if she looked at all like Ms. Winn. Carlotta watched and didn't say a word.

"Scram, Rosie," said George. "You're a waste, so we've heard, so don't waste our time. And by the way, did you have fun at school today? Did you?"

Rosie could feel the huh-huhs coming on again.

"This is my new, huh-huh, friend Carlotta," mumbled Rosie.

"Hello, Carlotta," said Bill. "I'm Bill."

"Look, George," interrupted Lizzie, "Rosie has helped us out a lot in the past. Maybe she could pronounce the words for all of us so we can all practice and have a turn at spelling the words. We'll be better prepared that way."

Rosie knew she should keep her mouth shut. If the gang let her help them, that would be a good way for *her* to learn the words and it wouldn't be boring. It might even be fun.

But Rosie couldn't keep silent.

"Mrs. Samuels says I have a marvelous speaking voice, just marvel—" trilled Rosie. Last week, when Rosie had made her voice trill, George had told her she sounded like a wounded bird. She hated that.

"I think it's a great idea to have Rosie be our pronouncer. Nobody here wants to read all those words out loud," added Helen.

"I accept," sang Rosie as she sat down and pulled her practice book out of her knapsack. Carlotta sat down too.

"Well, okay, Rosie," said George. "But if you mess us up at all, you're out. Get it? O-u-t spells out."

Rosie bit her tongue to keep herself from saying,

"I can spell *out,* you . . . you dodo!" She knew she had to be nice and friendly and pay attention and do a good job because if she was o-u-t, then she'd be *out* with George and the gang.

"Fair is fair," said Rosie. "One foul-up and I'm out, that is o-u-t out, George!"

"Rosie!" yelled George.

"Rosie, start pronouncing the words now . . . right now!" interrupted Lizzie. "And, George, don't yell at Rosie. We need her now."

Rosie started to pronounce the words. After about twenty words, she was having a great time. She was good at this and she knew it, and better yet, so did George. She was having so much fun.

"Now we're at the U's," trilled Rosie. She almost sang. She hoped she didn't sound like Ms. Mermin. *"Ug-li-fy,"* said Rosie in her steadiest, clearest voice. The word *uglify* made Rosie think of Ms. Mermin.

Rosie loved pronouncing all these words. Even though she didn't know what most of the words meant, they were still so much fun to say out loud. *"Umber, umpire, unabridged, undulate, unforgettable, unicorn, union, unique, university . . ."*

"Un-e-ver-si-ty," said Rosie.

"O-u-t!" shouted George.

"Why?" whined Rosie. "I've been doing a superb job."

"You pronounced *uni-versity, un-e-e-e-e,*" stammered George. "It's an *i*, not an *e*. I wonder how many other words you messed up and we didn't even know it, and now you've messed us all up!"

Rosie looked over at Lizzie for help, but this time Lizzie didn't say a word.

"Scram! You're out!" screamed George. "This isn't baseball . . . Rose Ann!"

Rosie always cringed when George called her Rose Ann. The only time Rosie was ever called Rose Ann, her formal name, was when she did something that would make her mom or dad or George really mad and say in a stern, loud voice, "Ro-ose Ann." She knew she was in trouble when anyone in her family called her Rose Ann.

"There aren't three outs in this game—only one!" George screamed again. "You're wasting our time. We heard about music class. Everyone knows Big Butt Mermin was right to . . ."

Rosie stood up and began to shout back at George. "Just you wait, huh-huh, George Davidson, just you wait! You're the one who's the pain in the butt . . . just like I said this morning. I'll win the spelling bee, the whole spelling bee, maybe even the All-American Spelling Bee-ee!" screamed Rosie as she grabbed Carlotta's arm and ran across the park, across Willard Street, into her house, and up to her room.

Rosie threw her knapsack on the floor.

"Hey," said Carlotta, "my brother used to treat me like that. Just forget it. You and I can study the practice book together."

"Great idea," said Rosie, who was beginning to feel calmer. But then she gasped. Everything—all her books and papers—had slid out of her knapsack. And sitting on top of all her books and papers was the list, the Top Secret list.

"That's the list I was telling you about," said Rosie as she pointed to it.

Rosie sat down on the floor and began to read the list to Carlotta. She had no idea what any of the words meant, but she sure loved saying them out loud—"*saponaceous, spoliator, xylography, vindaloo.*" Rosie sure wished the words would tell her something about the person who had left the list on the bench. She peered at the list. Maybe the words TOP SECRET! DO NOT READ! OR ELSE! would tell her something about the person. Maybe the list had to do with something special or secret that no one in the school was supposed to know about. She wondered why would someone print Top Secret on it. She didn't have a clue.

"Rosie, these words are much funnier-sounding than the practice-book words," Carlotta said as she began to laugh.

Rosie rolled over on the floor and burst out

laughing too. Then she bellowed, *"Vinda-loooooooooooo!"*

"Oh, no," said Carlotta as she looked at her watch. "I've got to go. My dad is picking me up here at five-thirty."

"Too bad," said Rosie. "This spelling stuff was beginning to be fun."

"If I were you," said Carlotta, "I'd put the list away and study from the practice book. That's what I'm going to do tonight. See you tomorrow."

Carlotta ran down the stairs and out the front door and into her dad's car.

Carlotta was right. She should forget about the list. Rosie stuffed the list back into her knapsack. Tomorrow she would sneak back to the bench and put the list back just where she had picked it up by mistake. She had to stop thinking about the Top Secret list and start thinking of a way to win the spelling bee. And she didn't have a clue of how to study for a spelling bee—at all!

Chapter
9

An-ti-dis-es-tab-lish-men-tar-i-an-ism

During math class the next day, Rosie found her mind wandering. Rosie's mind never wandered when she was in Mr. Lawler's room. She loved math. She'd always loved math. Rosie was in the highest math group. Her math group went off to a special room to meet with Mr. Lawler, who was head of the math department. But today during class with Mr. Lawler all Rosie could think about was spelling . . . and how in the world she was ever going to win her class spelling bee!

When math class was over, Rosie walked to her classroom alone. When she slid into her desk, she noticed that Carlotta was already sitting at her own desk and studying her practice book. "Did you practice?" asked Carlotta.

"Well, sort of," admitted Rosie, who couldn't

believe she had spent all evening after dinner reading the words from the Top Secret list. She'd even looked some of them up in the dictionary! Rosie wondered how she could have done that rather than study from the spelling bee practice book.

It bothered Rosie that she still had no idea what the list was about or why it existed or who had printed it out. It didn't make sense to her. Maybe it was some nerdy kid's secret computer game or secret code. She knew she *had* to return the list as soon as possible. It was beginning to cause her trouble.

At recess time Rosie jumped up from her desk, grabbed her knapsack, raced out of the classroom and down the hall, and plunked herself on Ms. Winn's bench.

Rosie looked up and down the hall. There was no one in sight. She quickly opened her knapsack, pulled out the Top Secret list, looked up and down the hall again, and slipped it under the bench. She sighed. She was glad she didn't have the list anymore.

The door to Ms. Winn's office opened and Ms. Winn stepped out into the hall. "Oh, no!" she said when she spotted Rosie. "You're not in trouble again, Rosie. I thought we had such a good talk."

Suddenly Rosie had an idea. She had a plan—

the beginnings of a new plan. Didn't Ms. Winn say her door was always open—that she would be glad to help anyone out? Well, Rosie did need help. And now she was going to ask for it.

Just then George and Lizzie walked by in their gym shorts. Rosie sure wished the entrance from the gym weren't right across from Ms. Winn's office. George and Lizzie stared at Rosie, but they didn't say a word as Rosie followed Ms. Winn into her office. Ms. Winn closed the door. She wasn't smiling. No wonder the kids thought she was a witch.

This time Rosie sat herself right down on the comfy purple couch and started talking. She liked it in Ms. Winn's office. It was fun in Ms. Winn's office. She'd never tell George how much fun it was.

"I'm not in trouble," Rosie blurted out. "I need some help."

Ms. Winn's frown turned into a smile. "How can I help you?" she asked.

"Well," said Rosie, "I need help to win the spelling bee. The only clue I have is Mr. McKernan's clue—to break up big words into smaller words. I don't have a clue how to practice for it."

"I'm so glad you came in and asked," said Ms. Winn. "You see, I had a favorite elementary school teacher whose name was Ms. Gabron, and she had a special technique for winning spelling bees. She taught it to me and I won my school bee one year.''

Rosie leaned forward. ''Can you teach it to me, huh-huh?'' she asked.

Ms. Winn straightened her purple glasses and answered, ''I sure can. Now listen, listen carefully.''

Rosie sat up and looked straight at Ms. Winn.

''You can relax,'' said Ms. Winn. ''Actually, the point of this technique is to let you relax so you won't be nervous and distracted and can concentrate on spelling the word correctly. Are you ready?''

''Yes, yes,'' answered Rosie, who was trying not to sound nervous.

''There are five steps to Ms. Gabron's special technique,'' explained Ms. Winn. ''Step One: When the person who's pronouncing says the word, take a deep breath and then look straight at the pronouncer and forget about anyone else in the room—the other kids in the bee, if there's an audience, everyone in the audience—block them all out. Pretend you and the pronouncer are the only two people in the room. Got that, Rosie?''

''I think so,'' answered Rosie, who wondered what was so special about that. She wondered if Ms. Winn could really help her out.

63

"Step Two," Ms. Winn went on to explain. "Close your eyes and picture the letters in your mind—picture what the word would look like if you were writing it down on a piece of paper. Make your mind actually 'see' the word in your mind. That's step two.

"Now Step Three: You spell the word to yourself with your eyes closed. Be sure it looks and sounds correct.

"Now Step Four: Take a deep breath and let the air out slowly.

"Step Five: You say the word out loud, and then you spell the word out loud."

"Oh," said Rosie, not quite sure if she understood what was so special about Ms. Winn's technique.

"Let's try it!" said Ms. Winn, who was so excited that she almost knocked one of the big piles of paper off her desk with her hand. "In my day," she said, "the big word was *antidisestablishmentarianism*. Stand up, Rosie. You be the spelling bee contestant. I'll be the pronouncer."

Rosie stood up. Her knees felt a little wobbly. She could feel the huh-huhs coming back. She knew she had to block out the huh-huhs at the same time she had to concentrate on what Ms. Winn was telling her, and wondered how she could do both.

"Now look straight at me," said Ms. Winn, "and block out everything else in this room. If the phone rings, ignore it. If someone knocks on the door, ignore it. Don't look at any of the pictures on the walls or at the flowers on my desk . . . or even the elephants!"

Rosie stared straight through her glasses at Ms. Winn as hard as she could. The huh-huhs disappeared! Then she took off her glasses and stuck them on top of her head.

"An-ti-dis-es-tab-lish-men-tar-i-an-ism," said Ms. Winn.

Rosie twisted a strand of her hair around and around. She took a deep breath. Then she closed her eyes. Then she said to herself, *"antidisestablishmentarianism."* Then she spelled, *"a-n-t-i-d-i-s-e-s-t-a-b-l-i-s-h-m-e-n-t-a-r-i-a-n-i-s-m."*

"You did it!" shouted Ms. Winn.

"I did?" asked Rosie.

"See! You can do it! You *can* win," said Ms. Winn in a softer voice as she leaned back in her chair. Rosie fell back onto the couch.

"You sort of go into a trance . . . into a spell . . . a spelling spell," uttered Rosie, who still did not believe that she had correctly spelled a word she'd never seen or heard before. Maybe she could win!

"There's one more thing," Ms. Winn added.

"You must study—which I assume you have by now—go over and over the words in the practice book until they are etched in your brain."

Rosie shuddered. She hadn't even opened the practice book. She'd spent all last night reading those stupid Top Secret words. Everyone else was ahead of her, George and his gang, Carlotta, even Kitty and Linda, probably everyone in the school. But she'd show all of them. She'd stay up all night and study, and she'd win.

"Good luck," said Ms. Winn as she opened the door to her office. "With all your hard work, I bet you'll be a winner. If you practice you can go all the way. You can be a winner, Rosie."

Rosie said thanks and raced out of the office. She took a quick peek at the bench. The Top Secret papers were gone. She wondered who had taken them. But she knew she had to stop thinking about the Top Secret list and concentrate on the words in her spelling bee practice book.

On Sunday Rosie spent the whole afternoon and evening studying her spelling practice book. "I hope I win my class bee," she told her mother. She didn't tell her mother that she didn't feel altogether crummy about trying to beat the new kid Carlotta. After all, if she didn't beat Carlotta, how could she ever win?

When Rosie explained to her mother that she

needed to stay up late and loved studying in the living room, her mother gave her permission to spend the night on the living room couch. At about ten-thirty Rosie began to feel very tired. She snuggled into her sleeping bag and fell asleep studying her words.

But she didn't sleep very well because she had a terrible nightmare. She dreamed that when she went to school the next morning, Mr. McKernan announced that the famous Willard Street creep, Mr. Quirk, Rosie Davidson's downstairs tenant, was going to be the pronouncer for their class spelling bee. And Rosie knew she could never, ever win if Mr. Quirk were around! What a nightmare!

Chapter

10

Either You Win or Lose!

The next day Rosie couldn't believe how slowly the day was going. She could hardly keep awake. She wished she hadn't had a nightmare.

By the time the spelling bee rolled around, Rosie could barely keep her eyes open.

"There are no winners and no losers in this spelling bee," said Mr. McKernan.

"Not true," mumbled Rosie to herself. "Either you win or lose. There's no in-between." Rosie made herself pay attention to Mr. McKernan. She stared right into Mr. McKernan's eyes. Rosie was amazed. She was waking up. In fact, she was beginning to feel wide awake.

"The winners of this bee," Mr. McKernan went on to explain, "in fact, all the winners from every class in our school, will go on to the citywide bee, and the winner of the citywide bee will be Boston's representative to the All-American Spelling Bee in Washington. Now I will pass this hat with numbers in it," boomed Mr. McKernan. "The hat has numbers from one to twenty-nine, the exact number of kids in this class. Everyone pick a number and line up according to your number."

Rosie crossed her fingers on her right hand and held her breath for good luck. She wasn't really superstitious or anything, but she'd heard on TV that if you cross fingers on both hands that's bad luck, and that holding your breath scares any evil spirits away—evil spirits like Mr. Quirk or George. Rosie put her hand into the hat, picked a number, and pulled it out. Then she let her breath out, slowly.

"What'd you get?" asked Carlotta, who sounded breathy too.

Rosie opened her hand and looked at the little piece of paper. On it was written the number thirteen. Rosie gasped.

"What's so bad about thirteen?" moaned Linda. "I got one. That's the worst. Imagine having to go first."

"No, I agree with Rosie," chimed in Kitty. "One is a lot better than having thirteen. Thirteen means bad luck. And one is at the beginning. Remember the saying 'beginner's luck'?"

70

"Quit all the yammering and line up. It's time to start," ordered Mr. McKernan. "And remember, I'll say the word, you repeat it, then spell it, then repeat it. If you misspell the word, you're out! If you're out, I'll ring the bell and you sit down. You will have done your best, and that's what counts. And no comments from the audience."

The first time Rosie was up she got the word *celery* and spelled it correctly. The second time she was up she got the word *chocolate*. Then she got the word *horseradish*. Rosie couldn't believe she was getting all food words. When she heard a couple of giggles, she tried to block them out. It was hard blocking everything out. But Rosie did notice that Kitty and Linda were out, o-u-t, out. In fact, when she finally took her eyes off Mr. McKernan, she was surprised that there were only three kids left—Nick, Carlotta, and *her!* Ms. Winn's technique was working!

Rosie's turn came up next. Mr. McKernan said *pretzel* and she spelled it correctly.

Rosie thought she heard Kitty whisper, "Good luck."

"Some luck," thought Rosie, "the luck of thirteen . . ."

Nick went out on the word *symphony*.

"Now it's nail-biting time," said Mr. McKernan.

71

"We're down to the final two. Now the rules change. I'll explain." Rosie could feel the huh-huhs returning. And she could begin to feel her hands shake. She had to do something. She took a big, deep breath. She quickly got her hands out of the way by slipping them into her pockets. Then Rosie straightened her glasses and stared at Mr. McKernan again. The huh-huhs disappeared. Her hands stopped shaking and sweating.

"Rosie is next, so she will get the first word," Mr. McKernan explained. "If she spells her word correctly, Carlotta will get a new word. If Carlotta spells her word correctly, Rosie will get the next word. If Carlotta makes a mistake on her word, Rosie will have a chance to spell Carlotta's word. If Rosie spells that word correctly, she will be given another word, and if she spells that word correctly, she wins . . . or vice-versa . . ."

Rosie smiled. She loved hearing the word *win*.

"Are you ready?" asked Mr. McKernan.

Rosie nodded yes and stared at Mr. McKernan.

Rosie spelled *extraordinary* correctly. She was so glad she didn't get another food word.

Carlotta spelled *science* correctly.

Rosie spelled *serious* correctly.

Carlotta misspelled *spaghetti s-p-a-g-e-t-t-i,* and Mr. McKernan rang the bell.

Rosie knew that now was the time to use her "Winn technique."

She took such a deep breath that she almost fainted. Then she closed her eyes and tried to picture how the word looked—what letters were in the word *spaghetti*. Suddenly her stomach rumbled and all she could see was a giant plate of piping hot spaghetti and meatballs. She couldn't see any letters at all! She started to panic. The huh-huhs came back. Soon she'd lose all her concentration and be a loser—just as George had said. Rosie put her hands in her pockets again and squeezed her eyes as tight as she could. Slowly, but surely, the big plate of spaghetti faded away and she could see the letters for the word *spaghetti* form in her mind. That was it! Carlotta had left out the *h*. At least Rosie was pretty sure that had been Carlotta's mistake.

"*S-p-a-g-h-e-t-t-i*," spelled Rosie.

"Correct," said Mr. McKernan. "Now you get one more word."

Rosie didn't dare take her eyes off Mr. McKernan. She fiddled with her watch. Then she twisted a strand of her hair around and around so hard it hurt. Her mouth felt dry. Finally she put her hands back in her pockets, closed her eyes, and calmed down again.

"*Zucchini*," said Mr. McKernan. "Some people love to bake *zucchini* bread."

Rosie hated zucchini—along with squash and

73

spinach and those awful little green vegetables, Brussels sprouts. Brussels sprouts once made her throw up!

But Rosie was glad she had gotten the word *zucchini*. A plate of piping hot zucchini would never pop up in her mind. Rosie closed her eyes. She said the word to herself. She wasn't quite sure of this word. Did it have two *c*'s or two *n*'s in it?

She kept her eyes closed as she spelled *"z-u-c-c-h-i-n-i."*

"You win, Rosie!" shouted Mr. McKernan, who ran over and gave her a hug. "On to the citywide bee, two weeks from this Saturday."

Rosie could hear her whole class clapping and could feel Kitty and Linda and Nick and Louie shaking her hand and saying things like "awesome" and "wicked." If this is what it felt like being a winner, she liked it. It sure beat being a loser. Suddenly Rosie remembered Carlotta. Carlotta was sitting at her desk all alone. She looked as though she were going to cry.

Rosie walked over to Carlotta and shook her hand. "I'm sorry you lost." Rosie was so glad she'd won, but she also felt bad about Carlotta losing.

"I'm getting used to being runner-up. That's what I was in Albuquerque," said Carlotta, who brushed a tear away from her eye. "At least I'm not a complete loser."

"You're a winner, too, and I need your help, huh-huh, I do. Will you be my coach?" asked Rosie.

A smile began to form on Carlotta's face. She nodded yes.

Rosie gave Carlotta a big hug. She could hardly believe that even though Carlotta had just lost, she had still agreed to be Rosie's coach. Carlotta was beginning to be Rosie's friend and Rosie was beginning to feel lucky.

All the way home from school Rosie couldn't believe that she was a winner. When she reached home, George and his gang were sitting on the front steps.

"Aren't you going to congratulate me?" asked George. "You're right. School is fun. I won my class spelling bee."

Rosie grabbed the railing of the front steps. She'd forgotten about George.

This time Rosie knew she had to concentrate and keep the huh-huhs from coming on. She put her hands on her hips and stared right into George's eyes.

"I won mine, too-oo," trilled Rosie in her calmest voice. "See you in two weeks at the citywide bee. May the best kid win!"

"Speaking of kid, you must be kidding," said George with a laugh. "There's no way you could win!"

Rosie wondered how she could possibly beat George. George had his whole gang to coach him! Mrs. Samuels was still out of town. And Rosie only had Carlotta. And that wasn't fair—at all!

Chapter

11

Winner Take All

During the next two weeks Rosie and Carlotta spent every afternoon and evening studying for the citywide spelling bee. Rosie had never spelled so many words. Even Kitty and Linda, who were at first jealous of Rosie and Carlotta, stopped by and took turns testing Rosie.

Every once in a while Rosie would look out at the park and see George's friends helping George practice for the bee. When Rosie did that, Carlotta would pull down the shades and tell Rosie to quit thinking about George. Rosie liked Carlotta and thought she was a good coach. But she wished Mrs. Samuels would come back from her trip. Mrs. Samuels had always been able to help out when Rosie was in a fix.

On Saturday morning, the day of the bee, Rosie felt as if she had a million words or more etched in her brain. George ate all of his breakfast. Rosie could hardly swallow a bite of hers. It made her mad that George seemed so normal, so calm, as if it were just a regular old Saturday.

After breakfast Rosie, George, and Mr. and Mrs. Davidson took the subway to City Hall.

When they reached the subway stop at City Hall Plaza, Rosie was glad to meet up with her friends Carlotta and Kitty and Linda and a bunch of her other classmates, along with Mr. McKernan. George's gang was also waiting for George, and he was glad to see them, too.

Lizzie whispered "Good luck" to Rosie before she joined George and the gang.

"Ms. Winn had to be away for the weekend," Mr. McKernan told Rosie and George. "She said to tell you both 'good luck.' "

When Rosie walked onto the brick plaza in front of Boston City Hall, she couldn't believe her eyes. Directly in front of City Hall was a big platform with about fifty chairs. Rosie hadn't realized that the bee was going to be held outside on City Hall Plaza. Once on the TV news, Rosie had seen the mayor give a key to the City of Boston to the president. She couldn't believe that she was going to sit on the very same stand that the mayor of Boston and the president had stood on. Maybe she didn't need to win this bee. Maybe just stepping and sit-

78

ting on the same platform that the president of the United States had sat on was enough. But then Rosie remembered what Ms. Winn had said to her. "You can go all the way. You can be a winner, Rosie." And Rosie knew she had to beat not only George, but also all the other kids, and go all the way . . . all the way to Washington. And that seemed like an impossible dream.

Mr. McKernan took Rosie and George to the platform and introduced them to Ms. Wall.

Ms. Wall, who told them she was a librarian and also one of the officials from the citywide bee, held out a hat and said, "Pick a number and then go find the seat on the platform that corresponds to your number."

George picked his number.

"I'm forty-seven," muttered George. "Well, good luck, Rosie," he added.

Rosie was startled. George sounded like he meant what he said. Rosie had forgotten that there were times when George was nice to her, very nice to her. He wasn't always a creep to her. Rosie thought that George sounded scared, too.

Rosie put her hand in the hat and picked a number. "Oh, no," she gasped when she saw the number. "I picked *one*. I can't believe it. I have to be the first."

"You'll do all right," said George. "Remember,

one is at the beginning. Remember beginner's luck?'' Rosie even managed a smile. George was being nice to her. And he was right. That's just what Linda had said when she'd picked *one*. But Linda had lost. Rosie wasn't sure anymore if being first was good or bad luck.

"Please take your seats, so we can start," announced Ms. Wall into the microphone.

Rosie found her seat easily and sat down. Even though there were lots of kids on the platform, Rosie felt so alone. Her parents, her friends, Mr. McKernan, and even George were all so far away from her. She never thought she'd ever miss George.

Ms. Wall explained the rules to everyone. Rosie knew them by heart and hardly listened to Ms. Wall. Rosie looked at the other kids. They all looked much older than she did. Maybe she was just the shortest. But being shortest didn't mean she was the dumbest.

"Are you ready for your word, Contestant Number One, Rosie Davidson?" asked Ms. Wall. "If you are ready, Rosie, please stand up."

Rosie could feel the huh-huhs coming. She knew she had to stop looking for her friends and put the "Winn technique" to work. Rosie stood up and stared at Ms. Wall. Ms. Wall seemed pretty pleasant to Rosie, so Rosie figured she wouldn't have any problem keeping her eyes on her for the whole spelling bee.

"*Artichoke*," pronounced Ms. Wall.

"Oh, no," thought Rosie to herself, "not more food!" Rosie thought she heard some giggles in the audience. She couldn't believe that her classmates would be so mean that they would giggle out loud and cause her to lose her concentration! Rosie was losing her concentration and she knew it! She knew she had to do something or else she would lose, and worse than that, she'd be a loser. "Step One," Rosie reminded herself. "Take a deep breath. Step Two: close your eyes."

Rosie took a deep breath and closed her eyes and put the "Winn technique" into gear and spelled *artichoke* correctly. Both Rosie and George spelled the next ten words correctly. Soon there were only four kids left—a kid named Linsey, a kid named Kusan, and Rosie and George.

Rosie could believe that George was still in. She couldn't believe that she was still in.

Rosie was beginning to feel tired. She crossed her fingers and prayed she wouldn't lose her concentration.

Linsey misspelled *ballerina* and was out. Rosie spelled *chimpanzee* correctly. George spelled *gymnasium* correctly and then Kusan misspelled *Olympiad*.

Rosie gasped. George gasped. And then Ms. Wall gasped, too, as she picked up the microphone

81

and said, "Would you believe that we're down to the final two? And that perhaps for the very first time in a citywide bee, we have a sister and brother competing against each other! This is spelling bee history! Remember, there'll be no loser here, just a runner-up, because the runner-up will also go to Washington. In case something happens to the winner, gets the flu or something, the runner-up will be a backup for the winner. But this will be a family trip no matter what happens!" Ms. Wall said with a laugh.

Rosie kept on staring at Ms. Wall. She was dying to take a peek at George, but she knew that even one small look would make her lose her concentration. She had to win. She didn't know if she could. Everyone always said George was a natural speller. She wondered how she could ever beat a natural speller. Rosie was beginning to feel very tired.

"Are you ready, Rosie?" asked Ms. Wall. Rosie nodded yes and closed her eyes tight. She was so nervous she thought she might just fall over in a faint. She wondered if that would make George win automatically. She knew she couldn't faint. But she couldn't even manage taking a deep breath. Rosie closed her eyes as tight as she could and spelled *puppeteer* correctly.

George spelled *rehearsal* correctly.

Rosie spelled *sledgehammer* correctly.

"George," said Ms. Wall, *"stegosaurus*. The *stegosaurus* was a plant-eating dinosaur."

Rosie knew George wouldn't misspell the name of a dinosaur. When Rosie and George were little, George knew the name of every single dinosaur and what they looked like. Rosie hated dinosaurs and couldn't care less about telling one from the other. At that age, all Rosie cared about was her collection of unicorns.

"S-t-e-g . . ." spelled George.

Suddenly there was a loud howl from the audience. George stopped spelling and looked out at the audience.

Coming down the aisle—with her dog Elmer on his leash—was Mrs. Samuels. Mrs. Samuels yanked Elmer with the leash and disappeared into a seat in the back of the plaza. Rosie squinted through her glasses, but she still couldn't see very clearly to the back row of seats. She knew that howl had come from Elmer. She'd know that howl anywhere. Rosie was glad she'd left Mrs. Samuels a note about the bee. Rosie's mind began to wander. It was going to be almost impossible to beat George, but with Mrs. Samuels and Elmer in the audience, she felt she had a chance.

Rosie stared at Ms. Wall. Even Ms. Wall looked nervous. Rosie thought she could hear Elmer moaning in the back row, but she didn't look out at the audience. She kept staring at Ms. Wall.

"*S-t-e-g* . . ." spelled George again. Then he paused.

"*S-t-e-g* . . ." George paused again. "*S-t-e-g-a* . . ."

"Sorry, George," said Ms. Wall as she rang the bell. "Now, Rosie, you get to spell *stegosaurus*."

Rosie jumped up and threw her fists into the air. Rosie couldn't believe George had misspelled the name of a dinosaur. She closed her eyes. She didn't dare look at George. For a minute all she could see in her mind were lots of white and pink and purple unicorns dancing around on a beautiful green field. She opened her eyes again and all she could see was George staring at her. She closed her eyes quickly and all she could see were hundreds of dinosaurs dancing around in some mud. Rosie took a deep breath. She knew she had to get back into her "Winn technique."

"Step One," she said to herself as she took a deep breath. Rosie said the word *stegosaurus* to herself. Then she tried to picture the letters in her mind. She thought she knew how to spell *stegosaurus,* but she wasn't sure. She didn't know whether the last letters were *u-s* or *o-u-s.* She knew George would know, but she sure couldn't ask George. She'd just have to go ahead and spell it.

Rosie opened her eyes and stared straight through

her glasses at Ms. Wall. *"S-t-e-g-o-s-a-u-r-u-s,"* Rosie said as quickly as she could.

"Correct," said Ms. Wall. "Now, Rosie, if you spell the next word correctly, you are our citywide winner, and you will go on to the All-American Spelling Bee in Washington."

The huh-huhs were back!

Chapter

12

Three Little Words

Rosie heard a cheer in the audience. It sounded like a combination of Kitty, Linda, Carlotta, and Elmer. Rosie could feel the huh-huhs coming on. She closed her eyes. She held her hands behind her to calm herself down. But nothing could stop the huh-huhs!

"Your word is *whippoorwill*. I will use it in a sentence," said Ms. Wall. "A *whippoorwill* is a bird that lives in the eastern, central, and southern United States. *Whippoorwill*."

Rosie closed her eyes and said "*whippoorwill*." She had no idea how to spell it. She'd never even heard of a *whippoorwill*. Was it spelled *e-r* or *o-r?*

She tried to picture the word in her mind. Then something amazing happened. She could see the word *whippoorwill* as three little words—just as

Mr. McKernan had said. She could see how to spell it.

Whippoorwill would be easy to spell. It was really only three words in one. *Whip, poor,* and *will.*

"*W-h-i-p,*" spelled Rosie. The audience was silent. Rosie could feel her hands shaking and her knees wobbling.

"*P-o-o-r,*" spelled Rosie, "*w-i-l-l.*"

And then she flopped back down in her chair and covered her eyes with her hands. She couldn't bear to look out at anyone, or anything, especially George. The truth was she couldn't bear to lose, to be a loser.

Something, she didn't know what, had made her think she'd made a mistake. After all, if she'd never even heard or seen the word *whippoorwill,* how would she ever have known how to spell it correctly?

Rosie felt someone gently taking her hands off her eyes, helping her, and taking her by the arm.

"Rosie, you won!" said Ms. Wall. "We are all so proud of you. You may be the youngest winner ever from Boston. Just how old are you?"

Rosie could feel her breath coming back. She was so excited that she could feel the huh-huhs coming back, too. But she didn't care. She had won! Who cared if a few huh-huhs slipped out now?

"I'm nine, huh-huh, nine-and-one-whole, huh-huh-half years old!" muttered Rosie.

Ms. Wall motioned to George to come up to the microphone and he did. Ms. Wall congratulated George.

Rosie looked at George for the very first time since the bee began. George looked very angry. She thought he would have looked sad because he had lost, or embarrassed because she had won. Didn't losers look sad or embarrassed? Well, how would she know, anyway? She wasn't a loser. George was. She was a winner! The winner!

"Now, Rosie, our champ, will you step over to the side to have your picture taken by our local newspaper the *Boston Chronicle,* which has organized and sponsored this bee."

"I'd love to," said Rosie.

Rosie smiled so hard for the photographer she thought her mouth would fall off. But she had never been in the newspaper before and she wanted to look good, real good. She told the reporter that her favorite activities were hanging out with her friends, Kitty, Linda, and Carlotta, and even at times with Nick and Louie, and helping out her brother's friends when they needed help, and doing math problems just for fun.

George had his picture taken after Rosie. Rosie walked down the steps from the platform, and

George followed her. Rosie thought George might have said ''Congratulations'' to her, but he didn't.

Mrs. Samuels, who was walking up the aisle, dragging Elmer by his leash, gave Rosie a big hug and kiss. ''Oh, my, Rosie, I'm so proud of you,'' she crooned. ''I knew you could do anything you wanted to do.'' Rosie looked at Elmer and started to laugh. Elmer had one of Mrs. Samuels' lace handkerchiefs tied around his mouth.

''When he howled I figured I had to stop him some way,'' explained Mrs. Samuels. ''I didn't want him disturbing any of the contestants. It wouldn't have been fair. And George, I must say, you did a fine job, too.''

''Elmer didn't do a fine job at all,'' shouted George, ''and he didn't disturb just any contestant. He disturbed *me!* And,'' George went on shouting, ''Rosie didn't win fair and square. Rosie rigged it so she would win. Rosie probably had one of her shrimpy friends step on Elmer's tail or something, and make him howl on purpose! Cheaters will do anything to win—anything! There's no way you could have won without cheating, Rosie!''

Rosie knew she shouldn't yell, that winners shouldn't yell—especially in public. But Rosie couldn't stop herself. She had to answer. She had to defend herself.

''You're wrong, George, huh-huh, you're wrong!''

she shrieked back. "One, I did not cheat! So I'm not a cheater. I won fair and square. Two, I didn't even know Mrs. Samuels and Elmer were back in town. It's true I left a note in her mailbox to invite her to the bee 'cause she's *my* friend, but that's all I did. And three," said Rosie, who could feel the huh-huhs go away and her voice calm down, "I won simply because I kept my concentration, and I beat you!"

"Cheater!" shouted George again. "You're a lousy speller. How could you win?"

"A win is a win, huh-huh!" shouted Rosie. "I have a win . . . a winning technique. I'll give you a clue." Rosie lowered her voice to a whisper. "I have a secret . . . a secret spell," she whispered.

"Rosie and George, both of you stop arguing this moment," interrupted Mrs. Davidson. "Daddy and I are so proud of both of you, we could burst! You are both winners, and better yet, we all get to go to Washington—a free trip to Washington. Now let's head into the subway and go home and have some lunch."

The next morning Rosie came down to breakfast before George. Her father handed her the Sunday edition of the *Chronicle* and pointed to the front page of the second section. Rosie couldn't believe her eyes.

There was a picture of her and one of George in

the newspaper. There was even a headline: LOCAL SISTER AND BROTHER ARE WINNER AND RUNNER-UP OF CITYWIDE SPELLING BEE.

"Wow!" said her father as he slid some pancakes onto Rosie's plate. "Read the part under your picture."

"'Winner, Rosie Davidson,'" read Rosie in a soft voice. She felt proud, too. "'Boston, Oldham Elementary School,'" she read on. "'Her winning word was *whippoorwil*. Her favorite activities are hanging out with her friends, helping out her brother's friends, and doing math problems. Her parents are Debbie and David Davidson.' Hey, the newspaper misspelled *whippoorwill*. They left off the last 'l.' They misspelled a word!"

"And you would have, too, if that stupid dog Elmer had howled when you had to spell your word," grumbled George.

George stood at the kitchen door. Rosie stopped reading and looked at him. He still looked angry.

"George," shouted Rosie, "I know you still think I cheated, but forget it, please. I mean, we're all going to Washington and we're both famous today. We're both in the newspaper!"

"Who cares?" grumbled George.

"I bet you do. It says right here, 'George Davidson,'" Rosie read, "'runner-up.'"

"I don't want to hear it!" said George.

"'His activities are soccer, piano, and karate. His parents are . . .'"

"I know who his parents are," whined George. "Listen, Rosie, you won. It was pretty embarrassing for me to have my little sister beat me. I know you won. So there. I hate to lose! So now that I've said it, can we stop talking about this bee? I'm sick of it."

"Okay," said Rosie, and she sat down and ate her pancakes in silence. She felt sorry for George. He really did feel bad. "You still get to come to Washington," added Rosie.

"I wouldn't come if I didn't have to," muttered George.

Rosie left the breakfast table. She didn't want to get into a fight with George again. She couldn't waste any energy on George. She had to call her friends to set up a coaching schedule. Carlotta had agreed to be Rosie's main coach. Kitty and Linda would substitute when Carlotta couldn't coach. Even Nick and Louie said they'd help out. For the next few weeks, Rosie's friends spent every afternoon and every other night quizzing her with words from the dictionary while Rosie paced back and forth across her room. One day Rosie was pacing back and forth so fast she walked right into her closet and Carlotta didn't let her come out until she had spelled the word *kerplunk* correctly.

93

Chapter

13

The Big Time

On the last Wednesday in May, Rosie, her parents, Kitty, Linda, Carlotta, George, Lizzie, Bill, and Ms. Winn arrived in Washington. As they were walking into the Capitol Suite Hotel, Rosie told Ms. Winn, "I have so many words crammed in my head, I feel like a walking dictionary!"

Rosie was very happy Ms. Winn had come to Washington, but she was really sorry that Mr. McKernan and Mrs. Samuels had not come. Mr. McKernan had to be at his brother's wedding and Mrs. Samuels had a bad cold. Rosie wondered if she could win this time without Mrs. Samuels and Elmer. She wasn't sure. This time *was* the big time.

On Thursday morning, the day of the bee, Rosie sat on the stage at the Capitol Suite Hotel and peered out into the audience. Ms. Winn had told her that rooms like these were used for big events—like dances and celebrations when there was a new president. Rosie figured every kid must have brought his or her family and friends and teacher and principal, and if you multiplied that by the two hundred fifty kids on the stage, there had to be at least two thousand or more people in the audience. There were even newspaper reporters and TV reporters with big cameras roving all over the place.

Rosie was seated in the first row of spellers, in the last chair on the far right-hand side of the stage. Directly in front of her was a microphone. "I bet that's the spellers' microphone," thought Rosie. "Thank goodness, I won't have to walk very far."

Rosie looked at the other kids. Some of them looked real brainy. No one looked stupid. She was excited that there were kids from all over the United States on the stage and that she was one of them.

For some reason Rosie didn't feel nervous. Perhaps it was because of the smooth stone she held in her hand. Mr. McKernan and her class had had a "good-luck send-off surprise party" for her and given her the beautiful ice-pink stone to take along as a good luck charm. Rosie cried when Louie said it was from the whole class and that Nick was the one who knew her favorite color was pink.

Suddenly the lights over the audience dimmed.

A tall man walked out onto the stage and over to the microphone.

"Hello, folks," he said. "I'm Mr. Rodriguez. I have the honor of being the head of the All-American Spelling Bee. I also have the honor of being here with two hundred and fifty of the best spellers in the land. This morning we have spelling bee winners from all fifty states." The audience clapped and cheered loudly.

"Now," Mr. Rodriguez went on, "that's the last clapping or cheering we'll hear, I trust, until we have a winner. We've explained the rules to the contestants. Now we want to explain rules to the audience. One: There shall be no clapping or cheering at all until the winner is announced. Two: We have to have it quiet so our contestants can concentrate, so if there are any loud disturbances, you will be asked to leave the hall and you will not be allowed to return."

Rosie rubbed the smooth stone. "This is getting serious," she thought to herself. "I'd better get into my 'Winn' mode—*now!*"

She stared hard at Mr. Rodriguez. He was pointing to the six adults who were sitting at a long table just below the stage. Two computers sat on the table, along with several dictionaries and notebooks.

"Let me introduce the judges," said Mr. Rodriguez, "Ms. Bellows, Ms. Ishimaru, Ms. McInnis,

Mr. Deletis, Mr. Sinicrope, and Mr. Moore. Usually we never have to handle any disagreements. But just in case someone disagrees with a spelling or the way a word is pronounced, we have a panel of six very distinguished educators ready.''

"Wow, this is serious stuff, very serious," thought Rosie. She still didn't feel nervous. She bet George was impressed. *She* sure was! She had picked number forty-nine. She wasn't at the beginning or the end, but just far enough along to watch a bunch of kids go before her. By the time her first word came up, she'd be ready. Everything had worked out "just peachy," as Mrs. Samuels liked to say when things were going well.

"And now, at the far left-hand side of the stage," said Mr. Rodriguez, "I'd like to introduce our grand pronouncer—the person who will pronounce the words for our contestants. As you know, our grand pronouncer is always a teacher, and always a very special teacher—someone whom students like and respect and someone who has a clear and distinct and, this year, beautiful voice. Every year our pronouncer has spent countless hours and days and weeks pronouncing billions and billions of words to prepare for this very day. Girls and boys, may I introduce Ms. Theodora Mermin, our grand pronouncer!''

"This couldn't be true," Rosie muttered to herself. "Maybe it's her daughter, or her mother, huh-huh, but it just can't be *my* music teacher!"

Just then Mr. Rodriguez added, ". . . from Boston, Massachusetts."

"No, it is her. I'd recognize her anywhere." Rosie continued muttering. "But something about her is very different, and I don't have a clue what it is!"

Ms. Mermin was sitting at a desk at the far opposite side of the stage from Rosie. A small microphone and several notebooks sat on the desk.

"It's her hair!" cried Rosie out loud. "Her silly bun's gone. That's it! She's cut her hair! That's why I didn't recognize her! But it's her all right, it's her! Actually, she looks pretty with her hair cut . . ."

The boy sitting next to Rosie turned and stared at her. Rosie tried to smile back. "He must think I'm bananas," Rosie thought to herself, "my talking out loud like that."

Ms. Mermin spoke into her microphone. "I am very proud to be here," she said in a clear and distinct voice. Rosie was very glad to be sitting so far away from Ms. Mermin.

"At least I'm as far away from Ms. Mermin as I can possibly be and still be on the stage," thought Rosie. "But how can I use my 'Winn technique' with Ms. Mermin, with someone who hates me, someone who thinks I'm a waste?" Rosie began to rub her good luck stone between her hands.

"If I can just get by the first word, I think I'll be able to stay in. Thank goodness, she's not wearing her glasses. I'll be so far away from her when I'm up at the spellers' microphone. She'll never recognize me without her glasses. It's my only hope."

Rosie figured it would be a long time before she got her first word. But before she knew it, she was standing up at the spellers' microphone.

Rosie stared straight across the stage at Ms. Mermin. Then she pronounced the word, closed her eyes and spelled *polydactyl* correctly.

Rosie ran back to her chair, flopped back down on it and gasped for air. Suddenly she felt calm. Ms. Mermin would be no problem. At least Rosie hoped she wouldn't be. "Probably," Rosie thought, "Ms. Mermin knows I'm in the bee and decided to forget about the past and treat me like a human being and give me a chance. Maybe . . . maybe not . . ."

Rosie spelled the next ten words correctly. She had no idea what *conglobe, drakelet, impofo, jodhpur, miljee, oxymoron, quiddity, raj, scabbard,* and *wiliwili* meant, but she was having fun spelling them.

Soon there were only three kids left. Rosie

straightened her glasses and brushed her hair off her forehead. So far, this had been no sweat.

The next kid spelled *zugzwang* incorrectly. He was so upset that, when he sat back down in his seat, he burst out crying, and one of the judges had to help him off the stage. Rosie felt sorry for him even though she didn't know him.

"Well," trilled Ms. Mermin into her microphone. "Now we're down to the final two, Troy and Rose Ann. You both know the rules, I do believe, so let's continue. Both of you, please go up to the spellers' microphone. Troy will have the next word."

Troy and Rosie walked up to the microphone.

"I'm the best speller in my state. I'm going to beat you! You're going to lose," whispered Troy to Rosie. Rosie didn't answer back. She knew Troy was just trying to rattle her.

"Tyrannize," announced Ms. Mermin into her microphone.

"Could you please use it in a sentence?" asked Troy.

"Please don't *tyrannize* Rose Ann," said Ms. Mermin.

Rosie heard someone in the audience laugh. She didn't think it was George.

"T-i . . ." spelled Troy. One of the judges rang the bell, and Troy stamped hard on his foot.

100

Rosie stared across the stage at Ms. Mermin and held her smooth stone, her good luck charm, tight between her hands. She was amazed that Ms. Mermin could still pretend not to recognize her. Her hands were beginning to sweat. She hoped her good luck piece wouldn't slide out of her hands. She needed to hang on to all the luck she could get.

"Tyrannize," said Ms. Mermin again.

"Tyrant," thought Rosie to herself. "No, that's not it." She closed her eyes. And then she blurted out, *"T-y-r-a-n . . ."* Then she took a deep breath. She had no idea if this was right or not, or if she should add another *n*. *"N-i-z-e . . ."* she said in a near whisper.

Troy stamped his other foot even harder when Ms. Mermin whispered "correct" into her microphone.

"This is it! The finale!" trilled Ms. Mermin. "If Rose Ann spells the next word correctly, she will be our next All-American Spelling Bee champ and go to the White House to receive a special award from the president—the president of the United States! If not, Troy will have another chance to win—to beat Rose Ann. Now, will the audience please quiet down for the benefit of both of our contestants? I thank you."

Rosie was amazed. She was fine. She was calm.

There were no huh-huhs. Her hands were not sweating or shaking. Her feet were flat on the ground. She was ready, ready to win!

"*Hibiscus*," said Ms. Mermin.

Rosie said the word out loud. She wished the word had been something like *vindaloo*, something easy. Then she closed her eyes. She could picture herself on the White House grounds, throwing a ball to the president and first lady's dog and looking out on the big street in front of the White House and seeing her brother peering in the gate, wishing he were where she was.

Chapter

14

Foul Play

"Rose Ann?" asked Ms. Mermin. "Do you want me to pronounce the word again?"

"Yes, please, huh-huh," said Rosie as loud as she could. Rosie knew she was losing her concentration and she'd better get it back.

"Hibiscus," said Ms. Mermin again.

Rosie took a very deep breath and closed her eyes even tighter. Suddenly the word appeared in her mind. Her mind felt like a radar screen, as if the word had popped up on a screen. Rosie could see the word, but she had no idea how to spell it. Her mouth felt dry. She licked her lips. Her hands felt sweaty, and her stomach felt as though it were doing flip-flops. Rosie wanted to sit down and quit. But she knew she couldn't. This was her chance to win, and she had to grab it!

"Can you use it in a sentence, please?" muttered Rosie.

"A *hibiscus* is one of the flowering plants on the White House grounds," said Ms. Mermin with a grin.

"*H-i,*" Rosie spelled. Then she took a deep breath and held on tight to her good luck charm. Was it an *s* next or not? She wasn't sure! She closed her eyes even tighter. She could hear Troy's breathing. She pressed her eyes so tight that they hurt and she pictured the word in her mind.

Then she said, "*b-i-s.*"

Rosie felt like fainting.

Then she said, "*c-u-s.*"

"Correct! Rose Ann Davidson from Boston, you are our winner, the All-American Spelling Bee Champ!" sang Ms. Mermin into her microphone. "Please take a bow. You, too, Troy—our runner-up."

This time Rosie thought she might really faint. She couldn't believe she had won. It was too good to be true.

Ms. Mermin gathered up her papers, put on her glasses, and stared across the stage at Rosie. Then she gasped. Then she stood up from her desk and practically ran across the stage to Rosie, who was still standing at the spellers' microphone.

"It is you, the real Rosie, not just any old Rose

Ann, and now you've won!" stammered Ms. Mermin. "It's Rosie . . . Rosie Davidson! When I was pronouncing all those beautiful words, I actually forgot it was you, that you were our Rosie from my school. I know that sounds crazy, but, you see, I was so nervous, I told myself I just had to concentrate on pronouncing the words correctly. So today when I first said your formal name, Rose Ann, I didn't even make the connection. I just forgot it was *you!*"

Rosie was speechless. She couldn't figure out what Ms. Mermin was doing. Why was she making such a big deal about herself when Rosie had just won?

"But now that I see and know it's you," Ms. Mermin went on to say, "and now that you actually won, I know that there's no way you could have won the whole bee fair and square. How stupid of me! I've been too fair to you, Rosie. I think there's been some foul play here. And I think I know what it is!"

Now Rosie really did feel faint. Suddenly everything that had happened made sense. Rosie knew what Ms. Mermin was thinking and she knew that Ms. Mermin was wrong. Rosie knew she'd won fair and square.

"Wait, folks. Don't leave the hall yet," shouted Ms. Mermin into the spellers' microphone.

"There's been some foul play, perhaps some cheating here with the winner. Troy, don't leave yet. You may be the winner after all, if it is true that Rosie Davidson has cheated and should be disqualified."

Rosie could not believe what she was hearing. She staggered over to her chair and flopped down. Her good luck charm slipped out of her hand and onto the floor, and Rosie didn't bother to pick it up.

"You see, I know Rosie," Ms. Mermin shouted into the microphone. "She's my student. She's from my school. When I found out that Rosie would be a participant in the All-American Spelling Bee and, of course, I knew that I would be the grand pronouncer and I had to keep that a secret, I told myself I had to treat Rosie the same as all the other contestants. That would only be fair. So, this morning, I almost put myself in a trance . . . so I could concentrate on the words and not on the kids who were spelling the words . . ."

"She's the real witch, not Ms. Winn, huh-huh!" muttered Rosie.

Mr. Rodriguez had left the judges' table and was up at the spellers' microphone talking with Ms. Mermin. Rosie knew now, knew too late, that her luck had run out. Ms. Mermin had had it in for her ever since she wrote that note in music class. And

Rosie now knew that the Top Secret list she had picked up by mistake must have been one of Ms. Mermin's lists for the spelling bee.

Ms. Mermin began to speak into the spellers' microphone again. "I'm afraid that Rose Ann Davidson must be disqualified and Troy Brown must be declared the winner. I was going to keep quiet, but I can't let cheating triumph. Even though it will bring shame to my own school, I must speak out!" trilled Ms. Mermin. "Rose Ann cheated!"

The audience was silent. So was Rosie. She wanted to scream out—to defend herself. She hadn't cheated and she knew it. How could Ms. Mermin accuse her? But no words came out of Rosie's mouth. Only the huh-huh's raced around her brain full speed.

"I must explain to the audience," said Ms. Mermin. "It's only fair that I explain. I feel terrible for our wonderful school, the Oldham School; our principal, Ms. Winn; and Rose Ann's teacher, Mr. McKernan; and Rosie's friends and classmates who have cheered her on every step of the way. This is a sad, instead of proud, day for the Oldham School."

There were so many huh-huh's pounding around in Rosie's head that she could barely hear a word

Ms. Mermin was saying. But Rosie knew it was bad—wicked bad—and she had no idea what she could do about it.

"You see," Ms. Mermin explained, "a few months ago, when I was chosen to be the grand pronouncer by the folks at the All-American Spelling Bee Headquarters, I was so proud. Teaching music is my first love, then my second love is the love of language, of words. I kept my Top Secret lists at school and any time that I did not have music class," Ms. Mermin went on to explain, "I would close the door and practice pronouncing the words so I could do an excellent job today. I thought it would only be fair to the contestants. One day one of my Top Secret lists—I had a lot of them—disappeared . . . the very list that had the word *hibiscus,* the very word Rose Ann won with just a few minutes ago. I had lots of lists, but I know that word came from the list Rosie must have stolen. I know that for a fact because that very list was quite wrinkled when I found it on a bench at school. I contend that Rosie willfully sneaked into my room, took my list and studied it, and then left it on a bench outside the principal's office where, by pure luck, I reclaimed it."

Rosie wasn't even paying attention now. She felt

109

so alone. She had no one to help her out and she didn't seem to be able to do anything to help herself out. She wasn't a winner anymore. She was a loser!

"I must confess, I was so nervous today that I didn't put on my distance glasses," Ms. Mermin went on to explain. "I need them only for seeing long distances, you know."

"She does look better without her bun," Rosie admitted to herself.

"I can't see across the stage without my glasses so I couldn't see Rosie clearly and I only addressed the spellers by their first names, so today I didn't even notice Rosie's or any of the spellers' last names. And I don't know Rosie as Rose Ann, the name I had on my list today. At our school in Boston, we call her Rosie. Well, put all this together, and I just didn't recognize her. I just *forgot* it was Rosie . . ." Ms. Mermin moaned. "I am so embarrassed to have caused all this trouble."

"You're embarrassed, huh-huh?" thought Rosie to herself. The huh-huhs had returned in full force. "What about me-eee!" she practically shrieked out loud.

Then Rosie noticed some commotion at the judges' table and she straightened up and peered through her glasses. Carlotta and Kitty and Linda were standing at the table and it looked like they were arguing with the judges.

Suddenly Kitty, Linda, and Carlotta leaped up onto the stage and ran over to Rosie. Linda told Rosie that they begged the judges to let Rosie tell her side of the story and that the judges had agreed to let Rosie speak. Carlotta told Rosie that she had to tell what *really* had happened to her, right now! Rosie had no idea how she got up from her chair, walked over to the microphone and started speaking. Her friends stood on one side of her while she explained. Rosie glared straight at Ms. Mermin, who was still standing next to the spellers' microphone.

Then Rosie spoke. "You see, huh-huh, you see, I didn't cheat, huh-huh. One day I was cleaning out my knapsack with all my school papers in it, and, huh-huh, I had to go in, huh-huh, to talk with Ms. Winn, our principal, and I picked up my papers and some others someone had carelessly left on the bench outside the principal's office by mistake. When I found the list in my knapsack, I didn't know whose list it was, huh-huh. It's true, I admit . . ."

Suddenly the huh-huhs disappeared and Rosie's voice came back loud and clear. "I admit I did read the list. I loved the words on the list and kept reading them over and over because they were so much fun to say aloud, and I discovered I loved

111

not just doing math and number problems, but I love words! But I don't ever even remember seeing that flower word I just spelled.''

Rosie hoped she wasn't shrieking, but she really didn't care anymore. She had to get out the truth.

Chapter
15

A Case of Carelessness

"I admit," Rosie said as a hush fell over the audience, "I did look at the list . . . a lot. But I didn't steal it. And I did put it back where I found it a couple of days later. And I never knew it had anything to do with any spelling bee at all! So this was not cheating!" And then Rosie lowered her voice. "And why was Ms. Mermin so careless as to leave a Top Secret list on a bench outside the principal's office?"

Rosie was on a roll now. She took off her glasses, stuck them in her hair and continued to glare at Ms. Mermin. Then Rosie pointed an accusing finger at Ms. Mermin, who glared back at Rosie.

"This is not a case of cheating! This is definitely a case of carelessness!" trilled Rosie.

Then Carlotta stepped up to the microphone.

"Rosie's telling the truth," she told the audience. "Ms. Mermin may not be proud of her, but we are. She's our best friend, and she would never cheat. It happened just like she said. Will the judges give her another chance? Give her another word off another list, a list neither Ms. Mermin nor Rosie has seen. If she spells the word correctly, she wins. If not, she loses."

It felt like hours before the judges made up their minds. Finally, Mr. Rodriguez stepped up to the microphone and announced, "The judges have agreed to let Rosie have another chance."

Then he opened his briefcase, pulled out some papers and held them up in his hand for all to see. "This is a list of words that no one but the six judges have seen," Mr. Rodriguez explained, "so there is no way anyone, Rosie or Ms. Mermin, could have seen the list. This list is a safeguard against cheating or cheating accusations."

Then Mr. Rodriguez added, "Yes, the judges have decided to give Rosie another chance to prove that she's a winner. But we think it's only fair that Troy be given another chance, too."

Rosie gasped.

"So we have a new list," Mr. Rodriguez went on to explain, "and Troy will be given the first chance to spell. If Troy spells the first word correctly, then Rosie will be given a new word. If

115

Troy misspells the first word, Rosie will be given
the same word, and if she spells it correctly, she
will be the winner. If she misspells that word, she
will be given a new word and the bee will go on
until either Troy or Rosie misspells a word and the
other then spells it correctly. The first person to
spell a word correctly after the other has misspelled
it will be the winner."

Rosie could barely concentrate on the rules. She
hoped she could concentrate on spelling.

"These two kids are such good spellers," Mr.
Rodriguez added as he handed the list to Ms. Mermin. "This could go on for days."

Rosie wasn't sure she could go on for another
second.

Before leaving the stage, Kitty picked up Rosie's
good luck charm—the smooth, pink stone—and
pressed it in her hand. "Remember, you're a winner," whispered Kitty.

"Remember, you're a champ," whispered Linda.

"Remember, pink's our winning color. You can
win, Rosie, you can!" whispered Carlotta as she
and Kitty and Linda raced off the stage.

Ms. Mermin asked Troy to step up to the spellers' microphone, and he did.

"I'm ready!" he whispered to Rosie. "This time
I will *tyrannize* you. I'm going to win!"

Ms. Mermin didn't return to her desk across the

stage. She stood right next to Rosie and Troy at the spellers' microphone.

Rosie's knees began to shake. She stared right into Ms. Mermin's eyes. This time Ms. Mermin looked scared and Rosie liked that. Rosie knew the stakes were high. She had to win to prove to Ms. Mermin, Ms. Winn, Mr. McKernan, her parents, Mrs. Samuels, George and his gang, Carlotta, Kitty, and Linda and all of her friends, to everyone she knew, that she really was a winner, not a cheater.

Now it was time to put herself into her "Winn technique." Maybe George was right. Maybe it was a trance—a witch's spell—a spell put on her by Ms. Winn. Maybe being a witch wasn't so bad after all, and that was something else she knew and George didn't. Rosie thought Ms. Winn was the best, and she knew a lot of other kids did, too!

Rosie took a deep breath and closed her eyes tight. She had to block Ms. Mermin out. She had to block Troy out. That was the only way she could possibly win.

"Troy, the first word is . . ." said Ms. Mermin, *"antidisestablishmentarianism."* Rosie couldn't believe her ears. This was the very same word Ms. Winn had given her back in her office when she taught Rosie the Winn technique.

Rosie heard Troy take the deepest, longest

117

breath she had ever heard anyone take. Then he started to spell. He spelled the word fast without stopping. *"A-n-t-i-d-i-s-e-s-t-a-b-l-i-s-h-m-e-n-t-t-a-r-i-a-n-i-s-m."*

Then Troy slapped his knee hard and yelled, "I got it right! I did it!"

Troy spelled the word so fast that Rosie had no idea whether he had spelled it correctly or not. Worse than that, she'd stopped concentrating.

"Good try, Troy, but you didn't spell the word quite right this time," said Ms. Mermin in a soft voice.

Rosie opened her eyes and looked at Troy. He looked as though he were going to cry.

Rosie put her good luck charm between her palms and rubbed it. She could see the word clearly in her mind. She didn't have to concentrate too hard. She didn't have to ask Ms. Mermin to use it in a sentence or pronounce it a second time. She didn't have to ask her to do anything. This was her word and she knew how to spell it.

But she closed her eyes anyway, this time just for effect. She wanted Troy to think she was in a trance. It wasn't over yet.

"*A-n-* . . ." said Rosie. "*-ti-dis-es-tab-lish-men-tar-ian-ism,*" she said as fast as she could.

"The contestant spelled the word so fast I'm not

118

sure I heard all the letters," grumbled Ms. Mermin. This time Rosie opened her eyes and glared at Ms. Mermin again.

"Oh, don't worry, Ms. Mermin," said Mr. Rodriguez. "That's just why we have our judges here. Rosie spelled it fast, but she spelled it correctly, and that makes her our winner for sure! Congratulations to Rose Ann Davidson, the proud winner from the Oldham School in Boston, Massachusetts."

Troy shook hands with Rosie. "Congratulations," he mumbled. "You won fair and square this time. I snuck an extra 't' in the word. That's what I did . . ."

Rosie told Troy he was a winner, too, and that she was glad he would be going to the White House with her. "I'm kind of scared to go alone, you know," she said.

Then Ms. Mermin shook hands with Rosie. "Congratulations to you," she stammered. "You're a winner."

Rosie and Troy watched Ms. Mermin practically run off the stage.

Suddenly Rosie realized that she was not just a winner, but that she had actually won *the* All-American Spelling Bee—that she had beat out two hundred and fifty of the best spellers from all over the whole United States! But no one had said that she would be going to the White House. It would be really disappointing not to meet the president after all she'd gone through.

Mr. Rodriguez ran over to Rosie. "Congratulations, young lady. You've been through a lot this morning."

Rosie didn't know how she managed to say "thank you," but she did.

"Now, Rosie," explained Mr. Rodriguez, "Right after lunch a special bus will be waiting at the front entrance of the hotel for you and Troy, and your teachers and family and friends, to take all of us to the White House to meet the president."

Rosie was so excited, she didn't eat one bit of her lunch. She left early with her mother and changed into her best sweater and skirt and a new pair of boots. "After all," she said to herself, "I *am* going to meet the president!"

Chapter
16

Roses for Rosie

At one o'clock Rosie piled into a large yellow
school bus with everyone from the bee who was
going to the White House. Just before Rosie got on
the bus, she spotted Ms. Mermin. Rosie looked at
her and felt a little bit sorry for her. She had made
a bit of a fool of herself. And she really was a good
music teacher, most of the time. So Rosie asked
Ms. Mermin to come on the bus . . . and she did.

The bus drove from the hotel down K Street,
turned onto Pennsylvania Avenue, and drove right
up the entrance of 1600 Pennsylvania Avenue.
Rosie gasped when the bus pulled into the drive-
way and Special White House Officer Berman
walked out of the guard house, unlocked the tall
iron gate, and waved the bus on through. The bus
stopped, and Officer Berman asked everyone to
come off the bus and follow the path. Rosie gasped

when she stepped off the bus and realized that the White House was right in front of her.

Officer Berman told everyone the awards ceremony was going to be in the Rose Garden, and that the president hoped he would be able to break away from his heavy work schedule to present the awards to Rosie and Troy. Everyone followed Officer Berman along the path. Rosie couldn't believe how beautiful it was at the White House. She'd always heard about spring in Washington, the nation's capital, but it was more beautiful than she had ever imagined. There were flowering trees and beds of flowers in full bloom in every color of the rainbow. Rosie had never seen grass so green. Rosie wished she could pick some flowers and take them home as a souvenir, but she knew she shouldn't.

She hoped her mom had brought film for her camera. She spotted her mom, and her mom, as usual, was taking pictures of everyone and everything in sight. Soon they reached a garden. The garden was full of hundreds of different shades of roses—red, yellow, orange, pink, white, and even purple roses. Rosie had never seen anything so beautiful in all her life. She was speechless. Then she realized where she was. She was in the Rose Garden—the exact place she had dreamed of coming ever since Ms. Winn had announced the spelling bee. There were about fifty chairs set up in front of a platform.

Rosie went to sit down with all the kids, when a woman came over and said, "Hi, I'm the president's press secretary, Susan Case. Will Rose Ann and Troy please come up to the platform? We have special seats for you. The president will be arriving shortly. Will everyone stand when he walks in—out of respect, please?"

"Oh, sure," said Rosie as she looked at Troy. Troy was smiling now and Rosie was glad. Rosie looked out at the audience. She saw Ms. Winn smiling at her. She bet Ms. Winn knew that Rosie had had a goal, to win a spelling bee—and that she had accomplished her goal, with a little help from Ms. Winn and her friends. Rosie found George in the crowd. Rosie wondered how George felt. She hoped he was having some fun.

"Ladies and gentlemen," announced Press Secretary Case, "the president of the United States."

Rosie jumped up from her seat and so did everyone else. Rosie was surprised. The president looked so friendly. Behind him ran his dog, a tan cocker spaniel named Dilly. Rosie thought it was probably a good thing that Elmer and Mrs. Samuels weren't there. Elmer would have howled and made the president of the United States lose his concentration! In fact, the president looked like a regular guy. And even with his full head of silver-gray hair, he looked a lot younger than he did on TV.

The president wasted no time. "I'm here to congratulate Rose Ann Davidson and Troy Brown. Troy is the runner-up in the All-American Spelling Bee, and I'm proud to award this plaque to you, Troy, for your excellence. Excellence and hard work are what America is all about. Congratulations, Troy." Rosie gave Troy a nudge on his arm and Troy stood up, walked over to the president, shook hands with the president and had his picture taken with the president!

"Now," said the president. "Rose Ann, you are the winner, the winner of the All-American Spelling Bee. You come right over here."

Rosie walked over to the president and looked up at him. Press Secretary Case handed the president a large gold plaque and a bouquet of red roses.

"Rose," said the president, "I present this engraved plaque to you on behalf of the All-American Spelling Bee as the winner—an all-American winner." The president stopped talking for a second. Then he said, "My, my. You are in the Rose Garden and your name is Rose, so it seems only correct that I present you with a bouquet of roses. Roses for—may I call you 'Rosie'?" asked the president.

"Sure," said Rosie.

"Then, roses for Rosie," said the president as he handed Rosie the bouquet and her plaque. "You know, I was my class spelling champ, but I could never get any farther than that. Tell me, Rosie, tell me the secret of your success.''

Rosie took a deep breath and stood up straight. "Well, you see,'' she trilled, "I have a secret spell.''

"You're not a witch or anything, casting spells or anything like that?'' teased the president.

"Oh, no,'' answered Rosie, "although sometimes my older brother, George, thinks I'm a witch. But anyway, my principal—she's here today—Ms. Winn, taught me the spelling technique that one of her teachers taught her and it worked for me. I call it the 'Winn technique' after my principal—that's spelled *p-a-l,* because she is my pal—and that technique made me win. Do you want to try it, Mr. President?'' Rosie had heard reporters on TV call the president "Mister,'' so she figured that's what she should do.

"Why, yes, sure,'' said the president.

"What you do is take a deep breath, close your eyes, and block everything out. Now, close your eyes, Mr. President.'' Rosie couldn't believe she was telling the president of the United States what to do. The president took a deep breath and closed his eyes.

"Now,'' said Rosie, "I'll say the word. You say it to yourself, then picture it in your mind, visualize

it, and then spell it. I bet you can do it. Are you ready?'' asked Rosie.

"Ready,'' said the president, whose eyes were still shut!

"Your word is *inauguration*,'' said Rosie.

"Well, I should know how to spell that one,'' said the president with a laugh, "but actually it's a toughy.''

"Now, don't talk, Mr. President,'' said Rosie. "Just do what I said.''

"Inauguration,'' said the president as he closed his eyes even tighter. *"I-n,''* he spelled, *"a-u-g-u-ra-tion.''* The president opened his eyes.

"Correct! You did it!'' shouted Rosie.

"You're a great kid,'' declared the president. "I have to go soon. Smile for the photographer. We've got to do this fast. My staff is waving me on to another meeting. I'm glad I got under your secret spell. You're a winner!'' Rosie didn't have any trouble smiling for the photographer. The president gave Rosie a hug and walked back into the White House. His dog, Dilly, and his staff trotted after him.

By the time Rosie walked back to the school bus, went to the airport, and flew home on the plane with everybody, she was exhausted, but happy. One thing surprised Rosie. George didn't say one mean thing to her. Maybe, for once, he was finally impressed with her and had some respect for her.

127

The next morning, at breakfast, Rosie couldn't believe her eyes when her mother showed her the newspaper. There, on the front page, was the picture of Rosie with the president, holding her roses and plaque. And underneath the picture, the caption said: ROSES FOR ROSIE—THE PRESIDENT'S WINNER!

When George sat down for breakfast, Rosie asked him if he wanted to see her picture.

"No thanks, Rosie," said George.

"But you've got to," whined Rosie.

"Look," shouted George, "you can't order me around like you ordered the president around."

"I can, too," answered Rosie calmly. "Want to hear my new joke that Mr. Rodriguez told me in Washington?" George covered his ears again.

"What's better than a dog that can count?" asked Rosie. George didn't answer.

"A spelling bee!" shrieked Rosie.

"I'm out of here!" screamed George.

And, as usual, Rosie and George were shouting at each other.

Rosie's List

Below is a list of some of the words Rosie and other characters in this book had to spell. Can you pronounce any of them? Can you use any of them in a sentence?

Just for fun, you might want to look up some of the other spelling words from this book that are not on this list.

You could look them up in your own dictionary. If they are not in your dictionary, you could look them up in a big, unabridged dictionary in your school library or neighborhood library.

I hope I didn't make any spelling mistakes in this book!

ROBIE H. HARRIS

antidisestablishmentarianism—a belief that is against the laws and customs of a community

bialys—large, round, flat baked rolls topped with onion flakes, orginally made in Poland

129

bocaccio—a large rockfish found on the coast of the Pacific Ocean

conglobe—to form in a ball

cupressineous—resembling a cyprus tree, an evergreen tree with dark, feathery leaves

impofo—an eland; a large African antelope with spirally twisted horns

kerplunk—a large dull sound with a thud

kookaburra—a bird from Australia that has a large bill and a call that sounds like loud laughter

mealymouthed—unwilling to tell the truth in plain or strong language

misericordia—forgiveness, kindness, sympathy, or compassion

Olympiad—an athletic contest held every fourth year at Olympia in Greece in ancient times, and revived since 1898 as an international athletic competition held every four years in different countries of the world

polydactyl—having more than the normal number of fingers or toes

profiterole—a miniature cream puff with a sweet filling

130

raj—a ruler; one who rules

scabbard—a leather or metal sheath in which the blade of a sword, dagger, or bayonet is enclosed when not in use

scribblative—writing that is wordy and hastily written

septuagenarian—a person seventy years old or between the ages of seventy and eighty

spoliator—one who robs in war

tatterdemalion—a person dressed in ragged clothing; a ragamuffin, a scarecrow.

undulate—rising and falling in waves

vindaloo—an Indian curry dish made of either meat, poultry, or fish with garlic, warm vinegar, and other spices and herbs

wiliwili—any of the soft coral trees found on the islands in the Pacific ocean and whose light, soft wood is often used for canoes

xylography—the art of making illustrations from wood blocks

zugzwang—when you have to make a move in the game of chess when it's *not* to your advantage.

131

About the Author

When author ROBIE H. HARRIS was growing up, she always wanted to win just one spelling bee, but she never did. Now when she has trouble spelling a word, she uses the "spell-check" on her computer, or looks it up in one of her dictionaries, or asks a friend.

Two years ago, she attended the National Spelling Bee in Washington, D.C., and had a great time interviewing many of the kids from all over America who participated in the bee.

Ms. Harris lives in Cambridge, Massachusetts, and is the author of picture books and novels for children.

Rosie's Rock 'n' Roll Riot is also published by Minstrel Books.

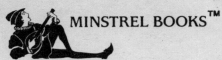